NOV   2007

Happy Birthday, Mrs. Piggle-Wiggle

OTHER BOOKS ABOUT OUR
FAVORITE PROBLEM-SOLVER!

Betty MacDonald
& Anne MacDonald Canham

Happy Birthday, Mrs. Piggle-Wiggle

ILLUSTRATIONS BY
Alexandra Boiger

HarperCollins*Publishers*

Library of Congress Cataloging-in-Publication Data is available.
ISBN 978-0-06-072812-0 (trade bdg.) — ISBN 978-0-06-072813-7 (lib. bdg.)

Typography by Amy Ryan
1 2 3 4 5 6 7 8 9 10

First Edition

Dedicated lovingly to my mother,
Betty MacDonald; my four married children;
their father, Robert Evans; my eight grandchildren
and two great grandchildren; and my niece,
two nephews, and their children.

Acknowledgments

I'd like to give a special thank-you to my daughter Joanie, who worked with me on this book side by side, word by word, never complaining. She was an inspiration, an excellent editor and critic, and made sense of my handwritten scrawl as she typed out the stories. Joanie not only listened as I read and reread each word I wrote, but also kept me focused on this project: "No, Mom, you don't need to go to the vegetable garden. You don't need to clean the chicken house. You need to sit, stay, keep writing! It's only 10:30, we don't need lunch yet."

Thanks also to Pal, Joanie's Australian shepherd, who sat at my feet, paws crossed, listening intently to each word while also making sure I didn't budge from my chair unless it was to get him a well-earned treat for his diligent supervision.

Thank you, Donald, my wonderfully patient, listening husband, for your endless support and enthusiasm. I love you.

Thanks, too, to my agent, Charles Schlessiger; the people at Brandt & Hochman Literary Agents, Inc., and Robert A. Freedman Dramatic Agency, Inc.; and my editor, Kristin Daly; her editorial assistant, Anastasia Cortez; and all the people at HarperCollins who believed in this project. Alexandra Boiger, your marvelous illustrations more than captured what Mrs. Piggle-Wiggle is all about.

My grateful thanks to everyone who has helped make this book a reality.

Anne MacDonald Canham

Contents

Happy Birthday, Mrs. Piggle-Wiggle

ONE

The Just-One-More-TV-Show Cure

The two Hanover children, Kitten and Sean, were in the living room watching television. Jack Timbertop the Forest Ranger had just caught the crooks who had deliberately set the whole forest on fire, intending to burn Jack and his brilliant, faithful police dog, Blaze, alive. *PUNCH! SMASH!* went the heavy fists of Jack Timbertop, and the crooks fell down unconscious.

Both Kitten and Sean breathed a big sigh of

relief. The brilliant, faithful police dog Blaze sniffed at the two criminals lying on the forest floor. Then he leaped up, put his two front paws on his master's shoulders, and barked right in his face. "Good dog, Blaze," said Jack Timbertop. Blaze whimpered and panted happily.

Mrs. Hanover, who was doing some knitting by the fire, called out, "Children, eight o'clock. Time for bed."

Sean, who was watching a commercial, pretended not to hear his mother. "Snappy Crackles! Jack Timbertop eats 'em on the show. They look real good."

"Very good," corrected Mr. Hanover, who was sitting on the couch reading *Field and Stream*.

"Well, very good, then," said Sean. "Will you get some tomorrow, Mom?"

"Not until you have finished the Marshmallow Oaty Crunch, Sweetie Pops, Strawberry Twirls, Frosted Fruity Puffs, and Cinnamon Apple Loops we got last week, and the week before and the week before and the week before," said Mrs. Hanover, sighing.

"Not fair, Mother," whined Sean. "Snappy Crackles are Jack Timbertop's favorite cereal."

"It's true, Mother," chimed in Kitten. "He says they're for real."

"Now just exactly what does that mean?" asked her father, shutting his magazine and slapping it down on the couch.

"Well," said Kitten, "I guess it means, uh, means, uh, they're delicious."

"Why doesn't he say so, then?" asked Mr. Hanover.

"Because he's a forest ranger," Sean quickly put in.

"I used to be a forest ranger," said Mr. Hanover, "and I never said cereal was for real."

"Maybe that's because you lived in the olden days," said Kitten.

Mrs. Hanover laughed. Mr. Hanover shouted, "Turn off the television! Turn it off!"

Both children wailed. "But Daddy, next is *Detective Danger*. It's the best show on television. Everybody watches it."

"Turn it off!" said Mr. Hanover.

Kitten threw herself on the floor and thrashed

around like a poisoned dog, howling and crying. Slowly, slowly, as though he were dragging a 200-pound anchor on each leg, Sean began to crawl toward the television set.

"TURN OFF THAT TELEVISION RIGHT NOW THIS MINUTE!" roared Mr. Hanover.

"Oh Daddy," wailed Kitten, "pleeeeeeeeeeeeez let us watch *Detective Danger*. Pleeeeeeeeez!"

"No," yelled Mr. Hanover. "Turn it off."

"But Daaaaaaaaaddddddy," sobbed Kitten, "every single person in my class watches *Detective Danger*."

"I don't care if every single child in the United States of America watches *Detective Danger*," growled Mr. Hanover. "*You* are going to bed."

"But not me, huh?" asked Sean hopefully, from his kneeling position in front of the television set.

"Yes you, huh!" said his father sternly. "*And turn that TV OFF now!*"

Sighing heavily, Sean turned the television off. Kitten rolled over onto her face on the floor and sobbed convulsively.

"Aw, stop your slobbering," said Sean disagreeably.

"You just be quiet," blurped Kitten, sitting up

and scrubbing her fists into her eyes. "It's all your fault we can't watch *Detective Danger*."

"It is not!" yelled Sean.

"It is so!" shrieked Kitten. "You asked Mom to buy Snappy Crackles and said they were real good and that made Dad mad."

"Aw, you don't know nothin'!" snarled Sean.

"Anything," corrected Mr. Hanover. "Now go to bed, both of you."

"Well, what time is it, anyway?" whined Sean.

"Five after eight," said his father briskly. "Now scat."

Sean slouched across the room and stood in front of his father. "How come we hafta go to bed at five after eight?" he asked. "All the other kids stay up 'til eight-thirty or nine."

"Children need their rest," said Mrs. Hanover gently. "It makes them big and strong, like Detective Danger."

"Well, how come they have *Detective Danger* on at eight o'clock then?" asked Sean.

"And then comes *The Wilson Family* (sniff) and after that is *Frisky* (gulp) and then comes *Johnnie*

Sanders (sniff), *Boy Detective*," said Kitten, who had gotten up off the floor and was leaning heavily against her mother's chair. "If we're s'posed to be in bed, how come they have all those programs for kids *after* eight-o'clock?"

"I'm sure I don't know," said Mrs. Hanover, putting her arms around her. "But I do know that your tears are splashing my knitting and you look sleepy."

"I'm not," said Kitten, rubbing her eyes on her sleeve and straightening up. "I feel perfectly wide-awake."

"So do I," said Sean. "I could stay up for hours."

"Well, you're not going to," said his father.

"And don't forget to brush your teeth," called Mrs. Hanover as the children slowly, reluctantly left the room and began to climb the stairs.

Mr. Hanover rolled his eyes up toward the ceiling and groaned. "Television! Ugh! Do you realize, Diana, that in another five years our children won't be able to speak English?"

"Oh, I wouldn't get so upset," said Mrs. Hanover calmly. "My father used to say the same thing about the comic books. He finally banned them from the house, and so of course we went over to the neighbor's and read them. However, the thing that bothers me is this haggling and whining and crying about going to bed every night."

Mr. Hanover said, "I wonder if all the other mothers and fathers in America are going through the same thing?"

"Not according to Kitten and Sean, they aren't," Mrs. Hanover laughed. "According to them, every single child in the United States but them stays up and watches *Detective Danger*, *Johnnie Sanders, Boy Detective*, etc., etc., etc. I wonder if they really do?"

"Why don't you call up a few of our friends and find out?" Mr. Hanover said.

"I think I shall," said Mrs. Hanover, putting away her knitting. "I think I'll call Millie Waxbean and see if Robin and Lark are still up." So she called her friend Millie Waxbean on the telephone, and who should answer but Lark.

"You're still up?" Mrs. Hanover asked.

"Yeah," said Lark. "We're watching *Detective Danger*. It's so cool tonight. Wanna speak to Mom?"

"Please," said Mrs. Hanover. When Mrs.

Waxbean came to the phone, Mrs. Hanover said, "Millie, I called because Hanley and I have just sent Kitten and Sean to bed snuffling and sobbing because they couldn't stay up and see *Detective Danger*, and I wanted to see if you let Robin and Lark stay up. I see that you have."

"Not without a struggle, though," said Mrs. Waxbean, laughing. "Bedtime around here used to be eight o'clock, but every single night it's the same thing. 'Oh, Mom, pleeeeeeeeez can't we watch *Detective Danger* or *Singing Sheriff* or *Crystal Maze* or *Space Rangers*? At first I was firm and made them go to bed, but as I got absolutely no help from Sterling, who says that discipline is the mother's job, I finally just couldn't stand the arguing and whimpering and whining that went on every night, and so I let them stay up."

"Aren't they tired in the morning?" Mrs. Hanover asked.

"They certainly are," said Mrs. Waxbean. "They are as cross as tigers with hydrophobia and start quarreling the minute they open their eyes. I wish I knew what to do."

Mrs. Hanover said, "Have you talked to any of the other mothers?"

"Oh, I talked to Harriet Hatchet, but naturally they don't have a television—she said that Hilary brought one home but Honor and Honesty made him take it back. They said it was foolish and noisy, the grammar was incorrect, and anyway, it interfered with their electronic or atomic research, or whatever the stuffy little bores do. Disagreeable as my children are, right now I certainly would not trade places with Harriet—those children of hers are like dreadful little miniature professors."

Mrs. Hanover laughed. "I wouldn't care if they had two heads if they didn't like television. Oh, Millie, what *are* we going to do?"

"Well," said Mrs. Waxbean, "just tonight I was wondering the same thing, and miracle of miracles, Sterling actually showed some interest in the problem, especially as we couldn't hear ourselves *think* over *Detective Danger*, and suggested that we call Mrs. Piggle-Wiggle."

"Mrs. who?" asked Mrs. Hanover.

"Oh, you know, Mrs. Piggle-Wiggle. That dear

little woman who lives in that upside-down house over on Vinemaple. I've heard that she is wonderful with children and knows all kinds of clever ways to cure their faults."

"But isn't she very old-fashioned? Would she know about modern things like television?" asked Mrs. Hanover.

"Well, I've heard that she knows *everything* about children, so she must know about television."

"Do you know her telephone number?" asked Mrs. Hanover.

"I believe it's in the phone book," said Mrs. Waxbean. "And if she has a cure for The-Just-One-More-TV-Show-ers, please let me know."

"I certainly shall," said Mrs. Hanover.

So Mrs. Hanover called Mrs. Piggle-Wiggle, and had just begun to tell her about Kitten and Sean and their always wanting to watch just one more program on TV, when Mrs. Piggle-Wiggle laughed and said, "Oh, I know all about it—*Detective Danger*, *The Wilson Family*, *Johnnie Sanders*, *Boy Detective*, and on and on. And all *after* eight-o'clock. It doesn't seem very fair, does it?"

"I suppose not," said Mrs. Hanover. "Especially to the mothers and fathers who have to listen to the whining and crying at bedtime."

"Of course, I don't have a television set," said Mrs. Piggle-Wiggle, "but I hear the children talking and I believe I know what the trouble is."

"What?" asked Mrs. Hanover eagerly.

"Oh, it's not that easy," said Mrs. Piggle-Wiggle. "I mean, I can't tell you what to do over the phone. I'd have to have the children with me for a day or two. Let me see now . . ." There was a long silence on the telephone, and then Mrs. Piggle-Wiggle said, "How would you and Mr. Hanover like to take a little trip and leave me with the children as a babysitter?"

"Do you really mean that?" asked Mrs. Hanover.

"Certainly I do," said Mrs. Piggle-Wiggle. "Provided, of course, I could bring Wag and Lightfoot. Lester is staying with the Eagers, so he's no problem."

"Of course, you can bring anyone you like," said Mrs. Hanover, who thought Lester was Mrs. Piggle-Wiggle's husband and Wag and Lightfoot were her children. "But our house is not too large."

Mrs. Piggle-Wiggle laughed. "Wag is my dog and he sleeps in the basement, and Lightfoot is my cat and she sleeps on the hearth."

"But who is Lester?" asked Mrs. Hanover, rather timidly.

"Lester is a pig," said Mrs. Piggle-Wiggle. "A very dear pig who teaches children good table manners, but as I said, he is staying with the Eagers this week so we don't need to worry about him. Now when would you like me to come?"

"How about Friday?" asked Mrs. Hanover.

"Fine," said Mrs. Piggle-Wiggle. "I'll be over right after breakfast. That way you can get an early start. By the way, where will you go?"

"To Lake Clearwater," said Mrs. Hanover. "That is where Mr. Hanover and I first met but we've never been back. It will be so wonderful to see that dear old rustic lodge again. Oh, Mrs. Piggle-Wiggle, you are so kind and I'm getting so excited. Just think, a trip! And no whining about television programs!" She laughed delightedly. "I can hardly wait."

Thursday night, Kitten and Sean were especially naughty. "I won't go to bed. I won't!" shrieked

Kitten when eight o'clock came. "*Montana Liz* is on next and I've *just got* to see her! I've *just got* to! She's riding in this rodeo and the prize is a beautiful trick horse named White Star and this mean guy is going to try and poison her horse, Pepper, and . . ."

"That's enough plot," said Mr. Hanover sternly.

"How do you know about all this?" asked Mrs. Hanover interestedly.

"Because every single child in school but us watches *Montana Liz*, that's why," Kitten yelled.

"Lower your voice," said her father.

"I can't!" gulped Kitten. "I'm too disappointed."

"Nonsense," said her father. "Go to bed. Now!"

Kitten hurled herself from the room and up the stairs, howling, "You're mean! You're bad! You don't love your children and you never want them to have any fun!"

Through Kitten's hysterics, Sean lay quietly on the floor watching television.

"Oh, no you don't," said his father. "Upstairs NOW!"

"That's right," Mrs. Hanover said. "I want you to take a bath."

"A bath!" Sean groaned. "Why?"

"Because you're dirty," said his father cheerfully. "Now git along, little doggie."

"I just had a bath, uh, uh, uh . . ."

"Two days ago," said his mother. "And I want you all nice and clean for Mrs. Piggle-Wiggle."

Sean jumped to his feet happily. "Hey, I forgot!" he said. "Mrs. Piggle-Wiggle's gonna stay with us. When's she coming, Mom?"

"She'll be here when you get home from school," said his mother. "Now kiss me good night. It's twenty after eight."

When Sean had gone upstairs, she said to Mr. Hanover, "Hanley, just think. This time tomorrow night we'll be up at the lake! Oh, I can hardly wait, not a sound but the lapping of the water on the shore and the crackle of the fire . . ."

"And if memory serves me, the whine of giant mosquitoes and the *smack, smack* of hands slapping at them."

"Oh, Hanley," Mrs. Hanover laughed. "You're so unromantic."

"He certainly is," came Kitten's voice from the

staircase. "He doesn't care about me."

"Come and kiss us good night," called her father. After he had kissed her tearstained cheek and blotted her swollen eyes and wiped her red nose, he said, "Do you really think that Montana Liz and her horse, Pepper, are worth all this?"

Mrs. Hanover said, "Poor Mrs. Piggle-Wiggle. I hope she knows what she's doing."

The next afternoon, when the children came home from school, Mrs. Piggle-Wiggle greeted them. The children hugged her, said how glad they were she was staying with them, then sat down with her to watch television and eat a snack of brownies and milk. It wasn't really a very good show—the good ones didn't come on until five—but Kitten and Sean watched it gladly because Mrs. Hanover never let them watch television when they first got home from school. She said they should play outside and get some fresh air into their lungs. Mrs. Piggle-Wiggle was wonderful. When Kitten and Sean finished their cookies and milk, she didn't even make them take the plates and glasses out to the kitchen. She said, "You just stay right here and watch your show."

When dinner time came, Mrs. Piggle-Wiggle brought them trays. She had one too, and they all watched *Dolphin Quest*, *Spy Dog*, and *Singing Sheriff*. Then it was eight-thirty. Both Kitten and Sean knew it was eight-thirty because that was when *Singing Sheriff* ended. They looked up at Mrs. Piggle-Wiggle, leaning back in the big green chair, crocheting a doily. Wag lay by her feet, Lightfoot was curled in her lap. Occasionally Lightfoot slapped at her crochet needle. Noticing finally that the children were watching her, she said, "Well, what's on next?"

"It's *Green River Gang*," Sean said excitedly. "It's a cool show. Lots of killin' and shootin' and robberies."

"Good," said Mrs. Piggle-Wiggle, "let's watch it."

"Oh, boy." Sean snapped to the right channel and turned the sound up good and loud.

Kitten leaned over and whispered to Sean, "She doesn't know it's our bedtime. Hee, hee, hee!"

Sean growled back, "Be quiet, stupid! You'll spoil everything!"

"Oh, no she won't," said Mrs. Piggle-Wiggle companionably. "I know that it is your bedtime, but this is Friday night and I'm in charge here, and your mother and father said that I could do just as I please. And I please that you should see all the television you want to while I am here."

"You mean we can see *Space Pirate* that's on after *Green River Gang*?" asked Kitten, her eyes as big as gumdrops.

"I do," said Mrs. Piggle-Wiggle, leaning down to scratch Wag behind his ears.

"And *The Lost Family* and *Jungle Tamers* and . . ." Kitten was breathless.

"*Late Night Cinema*," Sean finished triumphantly.

"*Late Night Cinema*," said Mrs. Piggle-Wiggle. "I've never seen it and I've always wanted to."

"Cool!" said Sean, getting up and giving Mrs. Piggle-Wiggle a hug. "You're the best babysitter in the whole world."

"We'll see," said Mrs. Piggle-Wiggle, smiling.

Well, they saw *Green River Gang* and *Space Pirate* and *The Lost Family* and *Jungle Tamer*, and then it was eleven o'clock and everybody was hungry, so Mrs. Piggle-Wiggle made cocoa and peanut-butter-and-banana sandwiches. While the milk was heating for the cocoa, Mrs. Piggle-Wiggle asked Sean to go down into the basement and get some more logs for the fire.

"Ya mean down in that dark ol' basement all by myself?" whined Sean, who had seen so much killing and so many robbers and crooks that he was almost afraid to open the refrigerator for fear there might be a killer in it.

"Are you afraid?" Mrs. Piggle-Wiggle asked.

"Well, no, not exactly afraid," Sean said. "It's just that this isn't a very good neighborhood, and Mr. Winter next door might be a jewel thief, and . . ."

"I see," said Mrs. Piggle-Wiggle. "In that case we'll all go and each carry up one log. Let's hurry because *Late Night Cinema*'s probably already started." So they hurried and brought up the logs and carried in the cocoa and sandwiches. Kitten went upstairs and got the comforter off her bed because she was sleepy but pretended she was cold. Unfortunately, *Late Night Cinema* was about forty years old, very dull, with old-fashioned-looking people. Kitten went to sleep before she had finished her sandwich. Sean went to sleep during the first commercial. Mrs. Piggle-

Wiggle let them sleep for a while, then she prodded Sean awake with her knitting bag. "Wake up," she said. "It's almost time for the *Late Late Night Cinema.*"

"Tha what?" Sean rolled over and rubbed his eyes.

"The *Late Late Night Cinema*," Mrs. Piggle-Wiggle said. "It's a cowboy picture." She prodded Kitten. Kitten snuggled down in her comforter. Sean gave her a sharp push with his foot.

"Owwwww!" Kitten screamed. "You kicked me. Mrs. Piggle-Wiggle, he kicked me."

"Oh, I did not," Sean said. "All I did was push you, you old baby."

"Whaaah! He hurt me!" Kitten howled.

"Now, now children," said Mrs. Piggle-Wiggle. "Let's not quarrel. After all, it's only midnight. We've got another whole movie to see."

"Midnight!" both children said in an awed voice. "Wow!" They livened up a little and began looking at the television. A woman in a white fox coat and short beaded dress was kissing a man. "Oh, mush," Sean said disgustedly.

19

"Never mind," said Mrs. Piggle-Wiggle. "This is about over. Why don't you run upstairs and wash your faces off with cold water to wake you up."

"Will you come up with us?" asked Kitten. "It's awfully scary at midnight."

"Oh, all right," said Mrs. Piggle-Wiggle. "I could stand a little cold water myself." *Late Late Night Cinema* was very good—herds of bison, hundreds of wild horses, lots of roping of steers, and hardly any mushy scenes between the handsome, young, brave sheriff and the stagecoach driver's daughter. But Kitten and Sean missed most of it. When one-thirty in the morning came and the movie was over, both children were sound asleep on the couch. Mrs. Piggle-Wiggle had to shake them pretty hard before they roused long enough to stagger up to bed.

Wag and Lightfoot were tired the next morning. Usually, when Mrs. Piggle-Wiggle's alarm went off at six-thirty in the morning, Wag came galloping up the basement stairs barking happily, "Good morning. Here I am. Let me out. I feel frisky." But this morning he was sleeping on an old blanket under Kitten's bed, protecting her from the killers she had been sure were hiding there the night before. Wag was terribly sleepy and couldn't believe his ears when he heard the familiar *rrrrrring* of the alarm clock. "It's probably only the telephone," he growled sleepily to himself, and closed his eyes.

Lightfoot, who was sleeping on Sean's pillow, guarding him from rattlesnakes, jewel thieves, and any stray criminals who might be loose in the neighborhood, heard the alarm, jumped off Sean's bed and up onto the window sill to see if there were any early birds she might scare. There were. A fat robin balancing on a branch of the maple tree right outside the window. "Cheep, cheep, cheep. Try and get me," he called impudently to Lightfoot, who was blinking sleepily.

"*Prrrow*, where are you?" Lightfoot asked through a huge yawn.

"I'm right here in front of your nose, silly," cheeped the robin, swinging the little branch back and forth. On the fourth swing he almost touched Lightfoot's nose. Lightfoot sat down and began washing her face. Then suddenly she put her head down on her paws and went to sleep.

"Well, I'll be darned," cheeped the robin. Then he dropped a big leaf down on Lightfoot's head like a hat and flew away.

Even Mrs. Piggle-Wiggle was pretty sleepy until she had had her first cup of coffee; then she felt fine. It was such a lovely morning. The early sunshine made little rainbows in Wag's water dish by the back door, and there were sparkles of dew on the daffodils. Mrs. Piggle-Wiggle took several deep breaths of the crisp morning air, then went upstairs to wake up the children. She tackled Kitten first. Gently she placed her hand on Kitten's forehead and said softly, "Kitten, wake up, it's morning and almost time for *Buried Treasure*." Kitten turned over on her side and buried her face in her pillow. Mrs. Piggle-Wiggle said a little louder, "Kitten, dear, wake up. It's morning." Kitten didn't move.

Finally Mrs. Piggle-Wiggle shouted, "KITTEN, WAKE UP!" Kitten sat up and said crossly, in a very whiny voice, "I'm too tired to wake up. I'm sleeeeepy."

"Of course you are," said Mrs. Piggle-Wiggle briskly. "You didn't get to bed until about two o'clock this morning, but if you want to see *Buried Treasure* you'll have to get up right now. Come on, scoot!"

She took Kitten by the shoulders and gently pushed her toward the edge of the bed. Stretching and yawning, Kitten started to lie down again. Mrs. Piggle-Wiggle took her arm and stood her up and pushed her toward the bathroom. "Go in and splash some cold water on your face," she said. "And hurry, it's almost seven."

"Seven!" moaned Kitten. "How come we're getting up so early? This is Saturday, you know."

"Yes, I know," said Mrs. Piggle-Wiggle, "but you and Sean wanted to see *Buried Treasure* and it comes on at seven-thirty."

"Oh goody, *Buried Treasure*. I forgot," Kitten stretched her arms over her head and yawned. "Is Sean up yet?"

"I'm just going to wake him now," Mrs. Piggle-Wiggle said.

Sean was stretched across his bed like the arms of a windmill. Lightfoot was curled on his pillow. Knowing boys, Mrs. Piggle-Wiggle didn't waste much time with gentle touches or whispering. She said in a loud voice, "Sean, WAKE UP!"

"*Zzzzzzzzzz*, don't shoot," mumbled Sean, his eyes tightly closed.

"SEAN, WAKE UP!" Mrs. Piggle-Wiggle had her mouth quite close to Sean's ear. He reached up and tried to brush her away like a buzzing fly, murmuring, "I'm all dressed, Mom. I just gotta saddle my horse."

Mrs. Piggle-Wiggle went into the bathroom, dipped a washrag in cold water, came back and washed Sean's face with it. At the first touch he leaped out of bed, eyes still closed, yelling, "Hey, whadda ya think you're doing?" Laughing, Mrs. Piggle-Wiggle put her arms around him and said, "Come on, Sean, wake up. It's almost time for *Buried Treasure*."

Sean blinked his eyes a few times, then began to sag toward the bed. Quickly Mrs. Piggle-Wiggle swiped at him with the cold washrag. He straightened up again and she pushed him toward the bathroom. "Now hurry," she said briskly. When Kitten came stumbling downstairs the *Buried Treasure* theme music was blaring. Mrs. Piggle-Wiggle guided her to the television set, sat her down, and handed her a tray with her breakfast on it. Two men in black wetsuits were swimming the murky bottom of the ocean floor, searching for a cave entrance.

Kitten turned to Mrs. Piggle-Wiggle and said crossly, "I think this is a boring show. Is there anything else on?"

Just then Sean ambled into the room. "Hey, I like this show."

"Well, I don't," sneered Kitten.

"WELL, I DO!" shouted Sean.

"It really doesn't make a difference what either of you think," said Mrs. Piggle-Wiggle calmly, rocking back and forth in her chair and sipping coffee, "because there's nothing else on but the news. Your breakfast tray's on the table there, Sean. Now let's settle down and watch TV."

They went through a string of programs and then it was time for lunch. The doorbell rang. Mrs. Piggle-Wiggle answered it but she didn't say who it was. Also, the telephone rang once or twice, but each time Mrs. Piggle-Wiggle answered. The first time it was Henry Fence and he wanted to speak to Sean. But it was right in the most exciting part of *Marathon Wrestling*, and so Sean told Mrs. Piggle-Wiggle to tell Henry he was busy. The second telephone call was Sylvia Quadrangle for Kitten, but Kitten was watching *Arizona Princess* and she told Mrs. Piggle-Wiggle to tell Sylvia she'd call her later.

During lunch, which they ate in front of the television, they watched a movie called *On the Trail*, then one called *Wagon Days*, then one called *Little Rustler*, then one called *Cody Cow Hand*, then one called *Heroes of the Tumbleweed*. During *Cody Cowhand*, Kitten dozed off. Sean slapped her on the head with the TV program magazine. Kitten hit him with the hearth broom, and then Mrs. Piggle-Wiggle said, "It must be bedtime."

"Bedtime!" both children wailed. "It can't be. It's still light out."

"It's always bedtime for quarrelers," said Mrs. Piggle-Wiggle, gathering up her sewing and snapping off the light.

"Oh please, Mrs. Piggle-Wiggle, let us stay up," pleaded Kitten. "We won't fight any more, honestly."

"Double criss-cross my heart," said Sean.

"Very well then," said Mrs. Piggle-Wiggle. "Sean, you build a fire in the fireplace, and Kitten and I will get supper ready. We're going to have hot dogs and baked beans."

"Oh boy, our favorite!" said the children.

When Sean went down to the basement to get the logs he heard Billy Ragweed and some of the other children playing Kick the Can out in back. He went out to see who was there and Billy called out, "Hey, Sean, how come you didn't come to Henry's party? You sick or something?"

"Henry didn't invite me to his party," said Sean sadly.

"He tried to," said Billy. "He telephoned you this morning like he did all of us kids, but you were busy or something. Gee, we had a great time at the party. His Uncle Cliff was there and he's a real live jet pilot. Well, I gotta go now. I'm it." Billy ran off down the street into the dusk. Sadly Sean went back into the basement and began filling the wood basket. Up in the kitchen Kitten was saying to Mrs. Piggle-Wiggle, in an accusing voice, "Why didn't you tell me that Sylvia Quadrangle wanted me to go to a movie with her?"

"Because I didn't know that," said Mrs. Piggle-Wiggle quietly. "All I knew was that Sylvia wanted to speak to you on the telephone and you were busy watching *Arizona Princess* and didn't want to be interrupted. You said you'd call her back but you didn't because another show came on. Now where are the dill pickles?"

Kitten got them out of the refrigerator and handed them to her quite sulkily. Mrs. Piggle-Wiggle didn't even seem to notice. She was busy taking out the baked beans and humming happily as she did so. Kitten ambled back into the living room. Sean was laying the fire in the fireplace.

Kitten said, "I'm so mad I could eat tacks."

"So am I," said Sean. "Henry Fence had a party this afternoon, and his uncle who is a real jet pilot was there."

"How come he didn't ask you?" Kitten asked.

"He tried to," said Sean. "He telephoned me when I was watching *Marathon Wrestling* and I told Mrs. Piggle-Wiggle to tell him I was busy and then

I forgot to call him back."

"Well," said Kitten furiously, "Sylvia Quadrangle and her mother wanted to take me to the movies this afternoon, and when *she* telephoned I told Mrs. Piggle-Wiggle to tell her I was busy because I was watching *Arizona Princess* and then I forgot to call her back."

"Oh well," said Mrs. Piggle-Wiggle, coming into the room and cheerfully putting down two trays of dinner. "It's a wonderful night for TV. What's on first?"

"*Magic Man*," said Kitten unenthusiastically.

"Sounds good," said Mrs. Piggle-Wiggle. "What does he do?"

"Oh, he flies around in the air and helps people," Kitten said yawning. "He's really kind of nerdy."

"He is not!" said Sean belligerently. "He's got X-ray eyes that can see everything!"

"Fine," said Mrs. Piggle-Wiggle. "I love X-ray eyes. Wish I had them myself. You find the station while I get my tray."

After *Magic Man* came *The Sheriff of Badlands*, then *Secret Service*, *Spy Dog*, *True Science Theater*,

Silver Bullets, *Navy Pilot*, *Bush Pilot*, and then *Late Night Cinema*. Kitten fell asleep during *Secret Service* and Sean during *Navy Pilot*. Mrs. Piggle-Wiggle let them sleep while she cleared up the dishes until it was time for the late movie. Then she called them, "KITTEN AND SEAN, WAKE UP!" Kitten squirmed around on the floor like a snake with a stomachache, moaning, "I'm so tired I'm sick. Leave me alone." Sean squinted his eyes tighter shut, buried his nose in the rug, and groaned, "I'm too sick to go to school, Mom. Honest I am."

Laughing, Mrs. Piggle-Wiggle leaned down and shook each child awake. Then she said, "Come on now, wake up. Don't be such sleepy heads. I want to watch *Late Night Cinema* and I don't want to sit here all by myself."

"Well, what's on *Late Night Cinema* tonight?" asked Kitten, scrubbing her eyes on her sleeve.

"Oh, it's a wonderful show," said Mrs. Piggle-Wiggle. "All about pirates and the Spanish Main."

"Oh," said Kitten, lying down on the floor again and closing her eyes.

"Aw, Kitten," said Mrs. Piggle-Wiggle in a very

whiny voice. "Pleeeeeeeease don't go to sleeeeeeep. I wanna watch *Late Night Cinema*."

Opening her eyes a tiny crack, Kitten looked at Mrs. Piggle-Wiggle and said, "But I'm sleepy. I don't want to stay up and see *Late Night Cinema*. I want to go to bed."

Then Mrs. Piggle-Wiggle said, "All you ever want to do is go to bed! I thought you loved television. If you go to bed, who will watch TV with me?"

Kitten sat right up. She said, "Gosh I'm sorry, Mrs. Piggle-Wiggle. I'll stay up and see *Late Night Cinema* with you." Then Mrs. Piggle-Wiggle leaned down and nudged Sean, who was lying on his back with his mouth open, sound asleep. "Wake up, Sean!" she said loudly.

Sean sat up, wiped his eyes on his shirttail, and said crossly, "Who poked me?"

"I did," said Mrs. Piggle-Wiggle. "I want you to wake up and watch *Late Night Cinema* with me. I don't wanna sit down here all by myself." Then she walked over to the fire and tapped Wag with her foot. "Wake up, old boy," she said. "Wake up and be a watchdog and keep the killers out of this house while we watch *Late Night Cinema* and *Late Late Night Cinema.*"

Wag woke up, growled at Mrs. Piggle-Wiggle, then walked over to Lightfoot, who was peacefully sleeping under Mrs. Piggle-Wiggle's chair, and snapped, "Wake up, you silly cat. Open your eyes and keep them open, we are going to stay up all night again watching television."

"Oh nooooooaw," said Lightfoot, switching her tail disagreeably. "Not again."

"Yes," snarled Wag. "The silly dummies."

Well, Mrs. Piggle-Wiggle and Kitten and Sean and Wag and Lightfoot did stay up clear through *Late Night Cinema*, but it certainly wasn't much fun for anybody. Sean and Kitten kept falling asleep, and when they weren't asleep they were pushing and shoving and saying rude things. Wag kept sneaking back to the fire and going to sleep. He might have gotten away with it if he hadn't snored. It seemed that every time there was something very exciting happening on television, there would come this big buzzing noise from the vicinity of the fireplace. The first time it happened, the pirates were just about to make the hero walk the plank. They already had him blindfolded and were about to lift him up onto the plank when suddenly they heard this noise like a bee in a tin can. *"Zzzzzzzzzzzzzzzz, zingzggggggg, zzzzzzz."*

"It's a jet plane come to save him!" shouted Sean.

"They didn't have jet planes in those days, stupid," said Kitten. "It's a speed boat."

"They didn't have speed boats in the olden days either," said Sean, giving her a push.

"They did so," said Kitten, pushing him back. "Only they ran with sails, so there!"

Mrs. Piggle-Wiggle said, "You're both wrong, children. The noise is Wag snoring and I'm going to tap him with my knitting needle and wake him up." She gently poked Wag with the dull end of the knitting needle, and he woke up for a little while but he was so cross and quarrelsome, snapping at Lightfoot, barking at Mrs. Piggle-Wiggle, and growling and snarling at Sean's bedroom slipper as if it were a wild rat, that they were really glad when he went back to sleep. Lightfoot was disagreeable too. She meowed and slapped at Wag and scratched Mrs. Piggle-

Wiggle when she tried to push her off her lap.

My, but everyone was glad when the television screen was finally dark and Mrs. Piggle-Wiggle announced, "Bedtime for everybody!"

However, just before she turned out the light, Mrs. Piggle-Wiggle took a last look at the program guide and said, "Cartoons at eight o'clock tomorrow! Who wants to get up and watch?"

"I don't!" said Kitten firmly.

"Not me!" yawned Sean.

"Lemme oooooouuuuuuut!" meowed Lightfoot.

"Keep it off off off oooooooof!" barked Wag.

"As a matter of fact," said Kitten stretching, "I'm so sick of television I could just die. Even if it rains tomorrow, I'm not going to watch it. I'm going to read and do my needlepoint and write in my diary."

"I'm going to go over to Henry Fence's house and see if his old jet pilot uncle is still there," said Sean.

"You want to know what I'm going to do?" said Mrs. Piggle-Wiggle. "I'm going to take two children named Kitten and Sean Hanover to Flack's Wild Animal Show and to dinner at Roy's Primeburgers.

And do you know why I'm going to take them? Because I promised their mother and daddy I would when they were cured of their Just-One-More-TV-Showitis. You are cured, aren't you?"

"We are, we are!" shouted the children.

TWO

The Won't-Brush-Teeth Cure

Betsy Applebee was a pretty little girl with a long, golden brown ponytail that came almost to her waist. Betsy's mother and father had always been extremely proud of their daughter and her sweet, ready smile, but lately they had begun to notice that Betsy's teeth were looking rather dingy.

One Saturday morning, Betsy hopped out of bed and hurried into her play clothes. The smell of cinnamon rolls came wafting up the stairs. Betsy loved cinnamon rolls and Saturdays. She always went skating with her best friend, Ellen. She raced downstairs to the kitchen, where her mother and father were eating breakfast and reading the morning paper.

Betsy wolfed down a cinnamon roll and a glass of milk.

Mrs. Applebee looked at Betsy lovingly. "Dear, I know you're in a hurry to go skating with Ellen today, but don't eat so fast or you'll make yourself ill."

Betsy was just about out the back door when Mr. Applebee called to her over the morning paper.

"Whoa, missy, where are you going in such a hurry? And aren't you forgetting to brush your teeth?"

"But Daddy, Ellen's waiting! Can't I brush them later, please?"

Betsy gave her father her most winning smile. He leaned forward with a piece of toast in his hand, peering at Betsy's mouth. "Wait a minute, what's that? Ugh! I think there's a kernel of corn stuck between your teeth."

Mrs. Applebee winced. "Betsy, really! Obviously

you did not brush last night. March upstairs and BRUSH YOUR TEETH RIGHT NOW. Ellen can wait."

Betsy stomped up the stairs into her bathroom, grumbling about the waste of time. She picked the corn kernel out from between her front teeth, put a smear of toothpaste on her toothbrush, made a few half-hearted swipes at her teeth, and rinsed with a tiny sip of water. The whole operation took less than thirty seconds, and when she reappeared in the kitchen before her father had time to eat his second bite of toast, he looked at her with raised eyebrows.

"That was fast!" he said suspiciously. "Smile at me, Betsy."

Betsy flashed him a grin.

"Well, you got the corn, at least," he sighed. "All right, go ahead."

Mrs. Applebee watched Betsy grab her skates off the back porch and race down the street toward Ellen's house. Then she turned to her husband, who was frowning into space.

"What is it, dear?" she asked.

"I'm just wondering," said Mr. Applebee, "how a

child can manage to eat an entire cinnamon roll without noticing she's got corn in her teeth."

"Goodness, that's a disgusting thought!" said Mrs. Applebee.

"My point exactly," replied her husband, returning to the morning paper.

That evening after dinner, Betsy was lying on the couch watching television when her mother came in to tell her to take a shower and brush her teeth.

"I'll dry your hair afterward," Mrs. Applebee promised. "And then, if you like, I can read you another chapter of *The Incredible Journey*."

Betsy loved this book. She ran up the stairs two at a time and in no time came bounding back down, all shiny and clean . . . except for her teeth, which she had only dabbed at with a wet finger.

When Mrs. Applebee finished reading the chapter aloud, Betsy was sleepily curled up by her side. Mr. Applebee bent down to kiss his little girl. As he did so, he winced at the smell of her breath.

"Betsy Applebee, you didn't brush your teeth!" Mrs. Applebee looked cross. "Go and do it now."

Betsy dragged herself up the stairs and into the

bathroom. She picked up her toothbrush, but then she caught sight of herself in the mirror. She liked the way her freshly washed and dried hair looked, all long and wavy down her back, and spent a few minutes admiring the effect from different angles. Then she turned on the water and waggled her toothbrush under the stream. She stuck it back in the holder and went to her room.

When her mother came in ten minutes later to tuck her in, Betsy was fast asleep. Mrs. Applebee leaned down to kiss her, but had to pull away because of the stench. Mrs. Applebee sighed.

"She can't have brushed her teeth," she muttered. But when she went to the bathroom to check, there was Betsy's toothbrush, still beaded with droplets of water. Mrs. Applebee felt guilty for doubting her little girl, and she went downstairs with a furrowed brow.

She found Mr. Applebee reading a book in the family room.

"Howard," said Mrs. Applebee. "I'm worried about Betsy. Her breath is terrible. I've heard, you know, that halitosis can be caused by illness. Do you suppose Betsy has some rare disease?"

Mr. Applebee laughed. "Not unless you consider laziness a disease. She's just got to start doing a better job of brushing her teeth."

"But Howard," said Mrs. Applebee, "I don't know what else to do. I nag her and nag her. Even a lecture from Dr. Pullit the dentist didn't help."

The next morning Betsy came happily skipping into the kitchen, where her mother was making Betsy and Mr. Applebee's favorite Sunday breakfast, French toast and sausages.

"Oh yum, I can hardly wait. I'm starving!" Betsy said as she slid into the chair next to her father.

Mr. Applebee jerked away from the smell of Betsy's breath and scooted his chair toward the other end of the table. He noticed that Betsy's teeth were now slightly mossy looking. Sesame seeds from last night's hamburger had lodged between her front teeth, along with other mysterious particles.

After breakfast, Betsy's father leaned back in his chair. "That was delicious, Florence. Now, Betsy, I didn't want to ruin our breakfast, but we have got to talk about your teeth. It's very obvious you haven't been brushing."

Betsy sighed heavily. "I know, I know, but I'm tired of doing the same old thing over and over. It's BOR-RING."

"So is sitting in a dentist's chair," said Mr. Applebee, "which is where you're going to be spending a lot of time unless you START BRUSHING YOUR TEETH."

"All right," said Betsy meekly, but that night at bedtime her father nearly gagged when she gave him a good night kiss.

"Young lady," he said sternly, "I detect the faint aroma of toothpaste, but if you brushed at all it must have been with a wet noodle. Those teeth of yours look as though they are starting to mildew. And your breath is just awful."

Betsy's mother said, "I wonder if it isn't that nervous stomach acting up again. You know how upset Betsy's stomach gets when she eats anything she might be allergic to."

"The only thing our Betsy seems to be allergic to these days is brushing those moss-covered teeth of hers," said Mr. Applebee.

The next morning, when Betsy came down to

breakfast, her mother asked her, "Betsy, did you remember to brush your teeth?"

Rolling her eyes, sighing heavily, and looking up at the kitchen ceiling, Betsy said, "I guess I forgot."

The look in her father's eyes made her remember in a hurry, and Betsy ran back upstairs. But later that morning, after Betsy had left for school, Mrs. Applebee checked her toothbrush and found to her dismay that it was completely dry.

She sighed to herself. "I'm going to call Sara Thorngate and ask her advice. Her children have beautiful teeth."

When Mrs. Thorngate answered the phone, Betsy's mother said, "Oh, Sara, I hope you can help me find a solution to a problem we're having with Betsy. I can't get her to brush her teeth. We have tried everything short of brushing them for her. And that seems foolish, considering she is eight years old."

"Oh, I disagree completely," said Mrs. Thorngate. "Jervil and I feel that the children's dental hygiene is *our* responsibility. We wouldn't *consider* letting our Rose, Jasmine, or Jervil Jr. brush their own teeth."

Betsy's mother winced. "But isn't Rose almost ten years old?" she asked.

"She was ten last March," said Mrs. Thorngate proudly. "And she's never had a single cavity. Her father brushes each individual tooth fifty times every night."

"I see," said Mrs. Applebee. "But won't that be impossible to continue when the children go away to college? Oops, I have to run, dear; something is boiling over on the stove."

She hung up abruptly, feeling even sadder about Betsy. Suddenly she remembered Betsy's little friend Patsy, who had hated baths, and how Patsy's mother had told her all about Mrs. Piggle-Wiggle and the magic ways she had of curing children's problems.

"Why didn't I think of that before I wasted my time talking to Sara Thorngate?" Mrs. Applebee wondered.

She found Mrs. Piggle-Wiggle's phone number. After a few rings, a cheerful voice answered, "Mrs. Piggle-Wiggle speaking."

"Hello, Mrs. Piggle-Wiggle, I'm Betsy Applebee's mother. Maybe you know my little girl. She loves playing at your house. She's always talking about your pets Wag and Lightfoot and how smart they are."

Mrs. Piggle-Wiggle said, "Of course I know Betsy! She is such a sweet girl, and what a lovely smile she has."

"Oh, that's just it, Mrs. Piggle-Wiggle," said Mrs. Applebee all in a rush. "Betsy is just as sweet as ever, but her smile isn't so lovely anymore. You see, she won't brush her teeth. In fact, I don't think she's brushed them in weeks. She walks around with food stuck between her teeth and doesn't even seem to notice. I'm afraid her sweet smile smells rather sour these days. I was hoping you might have a solution."

"Well, let me think a minute. Oh yes, I have a fine cure for Betsy. I'm certain it will work in a very short time. I think lots of children at some time or other forget to brush their teeth." Mrs. Piggle-Wiggle laughed. "Now, you don't object to dogs, do you?"

"Dogs?" asked Mrs. Applebee, rather taken aback.

"Yes, dogs. My dog, Wag, to be specific. He is very well trained and most capable with this particular cure I have for Betsy. Now, Mrs. Applebee, don't even mention tooth-brushing to Betsy for the rest of the week. Just tell her that she may take care of Wag for me this weekend. Betsy can pick him up at my house after school on Friday."

Mrs. Applebee said, "Absolutely, I'll tell Betsy. I can't thank you enough, Mrs. Piggle-Wiggle."

Mrs. Piggle-Wiggle added, "Now don't be surprised if Wag carries a little green satchel with him and puts it in the bathroom."

Mrs. Applebee said, "All right. Mr. Applebee will be delighted to have Wag for the weekend. We had been talking about surprising Betsy with a dog for her birthday, but the tooth-brushing problem has made us doubt whether she is responsible enough to take care of a pet. Oh! I almost forgot, what does Wag like to eat?"

Mrs. Piggle-Wiggle laughed and said, "Wag likes to eat most anything; he's not picky at all. Dog food, table scraps, bones. And cookies—especially cookies."

That night when Betsy went upstairs to get ready for bed, she was rather surprised that neither of her parents said a single word about brushing her teeth.

She ran a few drops of water over her toothbrush, hung it back up, and ran downstairs to kiss her mother and father good night. Mr. Applebee, who had heard all about Mrs. Piggle-Wiggle's instructions, hugged Betsy with his head turned away from her. Mrs. Applebee only gave Betsy a quick peck on her forehead, but Betsy didn't seem to notice.

The next morning Betsy didn't even bother running water on her toothbrush. After breakfast, when Betsy had left for school, Mr. Applebee said, "Florence, I can hardly stand to eat at the table with my own daughter. Have you noticed that food is sticking to her teeth?"

"I'm doing my best not to look," said Mrs. Applebee grimly.

"Yes, well, I'm doing *my* best not to breathe," said Mr. Applebee. "Mrs. Piggle-Wiggle's cure had better work, or we're going to have to start wearing gas masks just to kiss our daughter good night."

By the end of the week, Betsy's teeth looked like they were wearing a fuzzy green sweater. There appeared to be a raisin stuck between her two front teeth. Her breath now smelled so awful that her mother could almost imagine she saw yellow fumes coming out of her mouth.

"Thank goodness it's Friday," muttered Mr. Applebee after Betsy left for school that morning. "I can't take much more of this."

That afternoon, Betsy ran all the way to Mrs. Piggle-Wiggle's house. Mrs. Piggle-Wiggle and Wag were waiting for her on the front porch. In his teeth, Wag gripped a little green satchel by the handle.

When Betsy stooped down to give Wag a hug, he gave a little whine, because Betsy's breath was so awful. Wag looked up at Mrs. Piggle-Wiggle pleadingly. Mrs. Piggle-Wiggle bent down and whispered in his ear, explaining to Betsy that she was giving Wag some last-minute instructions.

"Oh, Wag," cried Betsy, kneeling down to pet him, "we're going to have such a great time together. I'm going to share my pork chops with you tonight."

Wag tried to hide behind Mrs. Piggle-Wiggle, flattening himself to the porch floor.

Betsy didn't notice. She just thanked Mrs. Piggle-Wiggle and assured her that she would take the best care of Wag in the whole world. Mrs. Piggle-Wiggle turned hastily away and buried her nose in a large rose that was blooming on the porch railing.

"That's fine, dear. You two have a wonderful time. My goodness, isn't this the loveliest climbing rose you ever saw?"

"Sure!" cried Betsy, tugging on Wag's leash. "I'll bring him back on my way to school Monday morning! Thanks, Mrs. Piggle-Wiggle."

Wag trotted ahead of her all the way to her house. Betsy burst in the door, shouting, "Mom, Wag's here!"

Wag politely offered Mrs. Applebee a paw. She shook it and said, "I'm very, very glad to have you here, Wag. Betsy dear, how would you and Wag like to have some milk and cookies? I baked your favorite, oatmeal raisin. Wag, you can have this nice blue bowl to drink out of."

Wag set his little green satchel on the floor beside his dish. Betsy offered him a cookie, which he ate in three neat bites. Then he lapped up the milk from his bowl and waited patiently while Betsy wolfed down three or four more cookies.

When Betsy had finished, Wag picked up his satchel in his mouth again. Then he began nudging Betsy toward the stairs with his cold, wet nose. Laughing, Betsy let herself be guided all the way upstairs and into the bathroom.

Mrs. Applebee followed. When she looked in the bathroom she stared in amazement. Wag had pushed Betsy's stool to the sink and was standing on it on his hind legs. His little green satchel sat on the rim of the sink. Wag snapped open the latch of the satchel with his paw and took out a red toothbrush and a tube of toothpaste. He held the toothpaste steady with one paw and very carefully grasped the cap with his teeth. After a few twists, the cap came off. Wag picked up the toothbrush in his mouth and held it next to the open toothpaste tube. With one paw he pushed gently on the tube, and a perfect dab of toothpaste squeezed onto the brush.

Then, clasping the toothbrush between his paws, he began to brush his sharp white teeth.

"Look, Mom," cried Betsy, clapping. "How cute!"

Mrs. Applebee watched with wide eyes. Every

now and then Wag spit delicately into the sink and then resumed his careful brushing.

"I didn't know dogs could spit," said Betsy.

"Neither did I," said Mrs. Applebee. "You certainly are a thorough brusher, Wag."

Wag winked at her in the mirror. Mrs. Applebee winked back and went downstairs to call Mr. Applebee at work.

When Wag had finished brushing, he packed everything back into his little green satchel. Then he looked expectantly at Betsy. He patted her toothbrush holder with his paw.

"My turn, boy? Okay," said Betsy.

She reached for her toothbrush and scraped a teeny bit of toothpaste onto the bristles. Wag growled and shook his head.

"More?" asked Betsy.

Wag gave a little nodding bark, as if to say yes. Betsy squeezed out more toothpaste.

"How's that?" she asked. She began to brush her teeth. At first she only gave a few weak swipes, but Wag growled again and touched her arm with his

paw. Betsy thought this was adorable, and she brushed a little harder. The raisin popped out from between her teeth and went swirling down the drain. Betsy stared at it in surprise. She spit, and more bits of food disappeared down the drain.

"Ick," said Betsy. Wag looked as if he agreed. He raised his paw to Betsy's arm again as if telling her to keep brushing. Betsy brushed until Wag took his paw down. Then she rinsed and spit. The water was clear, and in the mirror her teeth shone at her, white and clean.

Wag wagged his tail and sniffed happily at Betsy with his little black nose.

That night Betsy and her father had a fine time playing fetch with Wag. Wag sat up, rolled over, played dead, jumped rope with Betsy, shook hands, and thoroughly enjoyed his entire dinner, especially Betsy's pork chop. Betsy was so excited to have Wag visiting that she hardly touched her dinner. She didn't even have to be reminded to get ready to turn in for the night because of her mother's promise that Wag could sleep at the foot of her bed.

After Betsy had put on her pajamas, she went downstairs to say good night to her mother and father, then ran up the stairs, where Wag was waiting for her. Betsy hopped into bed and patted the foot of her bed for Wag, but Wag growled and crawled under the bed.

"It's all right, boy," said Betsy. "My mother said you can sleep up here."

But Wag went to the bedroom door and whined.

"Oh! I know what you want, boy," said Betsy. "We have to brush our teeth."

Wag wagged his tail and smiled his doggy smile at Betsy.

"I never saw a dog with such white teeth," said Betsy. "Come on, let's go brush."

A short while later, Mr. Applebee poked his head into Betsy's room. Betsy and Wag were snuggled in bed, and the room had the crisp minty toothpaste smell of freshly brushed teeth. Mr. Applebee breathed deeply.

"Ahh," he murmured, "I guess I won't need that gas mask after all."

"What did you say, Daddy?" asked Betsy sleepily.

"Nothing, sweetheart. So," he asked, "how do you like having a dog to curl up with?"

Betsy answered her father with a wide and gleaming smile.

THREE

The Insult Cure

"Yeah, well, you're a rhino-faced airhead!"

Blake Branson's voice shattered the peace of the quiet afternoon, startling his mother, who was folding socks in the laundry room. The back door crashed shut, and Mrs. Branson heard Blake stomp inside, still shouting.

"And you smell bad, too!"

Mrs. Branson glanced out the window and saw the retreating back of her son's best friend.

"Blake Branson, why were you yelling at Chuckie Keystop? He looked like he was about to cry."

Red in the face, and looking very defiant, Blake said, "Chuckie is just a big airheaded old crybaby. I don't care if I ever play with him again. He's a dummy."

"Why, Blake!" gasped Mrs. Branson, dropping the socks and storming into the kitchen, where Blake was throwing cabinet doors open in search of a snack. "It's not like you to say such horrid things to your friend. I hope you're going to apologize."

"Why should I apologize to a crybaby?" retorted Blake. "Everything I said was true. He *is* a crybaby, and he does have a nose like a rhino."

"Well, that doesn't mean you should point it out," said Mrs. Branson.

"But it's funny!" Blake protested.

"I didn't hear Chuckie laughing," Mrs. Branson snapped. "You march up to your room, young man, and think about how you hurt people's feelings when you say unkind things."

Blake sulked out of the kitchen and went up to his room, where the only thing he thought about was more "funny" things to say. In fact, he got out a piece of paper and began to write them down.

By dinnertime, the list had grown quite long. Blake's hand was tired from writing but he felt a warm sense of accomplishment. He had come up with what he felt were some truly hilarious insults, and he couldn't wait to try them out. He heard voices outside his bedroom window and looked out to see the three Gray children walking down the street.

"Hey, you snaggle-toothed, eagle-beaked dim-wits!"

"BLAKE BRANSON!" roared his father's voice behind him.

Blake jumped and whirled around. Mr. Branson was standing in the doorway, looking very angry.

"Seems to me," said Mr. Branson through gritted teeth, "that the dimwit is the one yelling the insults out the window at unsuspecting passersby."

Blake gulped.

Mr. Branson went on. "Your mother told me about what you said to Chuckie Keystop. If you continue to say mean things, son, you won't have a single friend left in the whole school. Now come on downstairs and eat your dinner."

Supper was a very quiet affair in the Branson household that night, even though Blake's mother had made his favorite, pot roast. Mrs. Branson was too upset to speak, Mr. Branson was too angry, and Blake was too busy thinking up new insults. After dinner he went back to his room and added them to his list, which he then shoved under some books on his desk.

Mrs. Branson found it there the next morning after Blake had left for school. She read:

four eyes
slop head
dimwit
duck feet
cow eyes
pig eyes
dog eyes
brace face
rake teeth
smelly head
rat face
spitty lips

snaggle tooth
mush mouth
dog breath
horse face
bird brain
bug eyes

Poor Mrs. Branson was more upset than ever. She went to the kitchen, poured herself a cup of tea, and sat staring at Blake's list. After a few minutes she picked up the phone and dialed her friend Mrs. Goodwin.

"Oh, Gertrude, I don't know what to do. Blake has developed the most awful mouth. He's always saying mean things to people, and just now I actually found a list of all the insults he's dreamed up!"

"You poor dear," clucked Mrs. Goodwin. "I feel so sorry for you. Why just last night I was telling Worthmont that Blake had been extremely insulting to our darling little children at school yesterday. He called our dear little Percival a hog face and he called Prissy and Candace fat, cow-eyed dummies."

Mrs. Branson groaned. "I'm so very, very sorry,

Gertrude. I'll deal with Blake as soon as he comes home from school."

"I would appreciate that, Bernice," said Mrs. Goodwin emphatically. "Percival was in tears over it, the poor little thing. It isn't his fault his nose turns up at the end. Of course *some* people think upturned noses are the most attractive kind of noses, but I suppose a little boy like Blake can't be expected to know that."

"No, I suppose not." Mrs. Branson sighed, thinking privately that Percival Goodwin's nose did look rather like a pig's snout. But still, she told herself sternly, that didn't excuse Blake's saying so. She apologized once more to Mrs. Goodwin and hung up the phone.

When Blake came home from school that afternoon he said, "Mrs. Moonface sent home a note for you, Mom."

"Blake!" cried Mrs. Branson. "I will *not* have you calling your teacher names. Mrs. Mooney is a very nice woman and a fine teacher."

She sighed and unfolded the note.

It said:

Dear Mrs. Branson,

I don't know what to think of Blake's behavior toward his classmates. Blake is a very good student and was very kind at the beginning of the term. But now he says so many mean things that he is alienating himself from most of the class. I suggest that you call Mrs. Piggle-Wiggle. She has cured so many children of some of the worst habits. Let me know if I can be of further help.

Sincerely,
Elizabeth Mooney

Mrs. Branson put the note on the kitchen bulletin board. Then she sent Blake up to his room to do his homework.

"You are to stay in your room until your father comes home. This mean streak you have developed *must end.*"

Blake stalked off, muttering under his breath.

". . . Old crab patch . . ."

"What did you say?" demanded his mother.

"Nothing, Mom," said Blake, hastily retreating to his room.

As soon as he was gone, his mother called Mrs. Piggle-Wiggle. When Mrs. Piggle-Wiggle answered "Hello" in her cheery voice, Mrs. Branson said, "Oh, Mrs. Piggle-Wiggle, this is Blake Branson's mother."

Mrs. Piggle-Wiggle laughed merrily. "Oh, hello, Mrs. Branson. I wondered if you'd be getting in touch. I've been hearing about Blake from the other children. Some of them apparently think he's quite funny . . . but only if he's making fun of someone else, of course. I gather he has developed quite a sharp tongue."

"He certainly has," said Mrs. Branson. "I even got a note from his teacher today—and I won't tell you what he said about *her*. I really don't understand what has happened to him. He used to be such a sweet boy."

Mrs. Piggle-Wiggle laughed again. "Well, perhaps I can help. Tell Blake to stop here on his way home from school tomorrow to pick up a package. It will be rather heavy, but Blake is a strong boy. Don't bother to say anything to Blake about his mean remarks. After dinner tomorrow, let Blake open the package and read the instructions. I imagine you'll see good results by the end of the week."

When Mr. Branson came home, he found his wife humming happily as she fixed dinner.

"Well, this is a welcome change," he said. "Has our smart-mouthed son mended his ways?"

"Oh, no, quite the contrary," said Mrs. Branson placidly. "In fact, he's worse than ever. But don't worry, Norman—help is on the way."

The next day at breakfast, Mrs. Branson told Blake to stop by Mrs. Piggle-Wiggle's house after school and pick up a package.

"Sure, Mom," said Blake, running out the door. Mrs. Branson heard him yelling at Larry Gray, "Hey, lizard lips, wait up!"

That afternoon Blake came staggering in the back door carrying a large package.

"Wow, this sure is heavy. I wanted to borrow Dick Thompson's wagon to haul this in but he said, 'No way, Blake, you're just too mean.' So I called him a rat-faced moron." Blake doubled over in laughter at his own wit.

Mrs. Branson didn't laugh. She took the package and set it on the kitchen table. She was tempted to peek inside, but she didn't want to risk interfering with Mrs. Piggle-Wiggle's cure. But Blake noticed that dinner was served very early that evening.

As soon as the plates were cleared, Mrs. Branson said, "Now let's see what's in this package from Mrs. Piggle-Wiggle."

Mr. Branson carefully untied the heavy twine, unwrapping a very large stack of black paper with ragged edges, a fat pen marked "Magic Glow-in-the-Dark Pen," and a note addressed to Blake from Mrs. Piggle-Wiggle.

Dear Blake,

Write down every insult you say each day before you go to bed at night.

Good Luck,

Mrs. Piggle-Wiggle

"Cool!" Blake shouted. He carried the paper and pen up to his room and put it on his desk. Then he took the first sheet of black, ragged-edged paper from the pile and wrote "lizard lips" with the special pen. The ink was white and faintly luminous.

"Wow, it glows!" Blake said excitedly. Suddenly the piece of paper fluttered into the air. Blake shouted in surprise and watched as the paper floated up to the ceiling. It hovered there, above his bed, the words "lizard lips" glowing off the page.

"This is the coolest thing ever," Blake whispered in awe. He reached eagerly for another sheet of the black paper.

"Rat-faced moron," he wrote, and to his delight, this paper too fluttered off the desk to hover just below the ceiling. Before long the ceiling over his bed was covered with dozens of ragged-edged black pages, each of them emblazoned with a glowing white insult. The room was lit up by the luminous scrawls.

Blake's father poked his head into the room. He caught sight of the fluttering papers and stared for a very long time, his eyes wide and thoughtful.

"Well, son," he murmured, "keep this up and you won't need to turn on any lights in this room." Mr. Branson cleared his throat. "I think that's enough writing for tonight, Blake. Time to get ready for bed."

When he came into the kitchen where his wife was finishing the dinner dishes, he said weakly, "Bernice, I wouldn't believe it if I hadn't seen it with my own two eyes."

He described the floating black pages with their white words shining down on Blake's bed. "It's like a Milky Way of insults!"

The next morning Blake looked a little sleepy when he sat down to eat his breakfast, and he couldn't stop yawning.

His father looked at Blake over the morning paper. "Eat your breakfast, son. I'll give you a ride today. You look a little too tired to walk to school."

Blake could barely keep his eyes open in class, and in fact Mrs. Mooney had to prod him gently to wake up twice. As Blake came slowly home from school, dragging his feet, he was almost too tired to yell mean things at Kitty Wheeling and Molly O'Toole when they ran giggling past him. But Molly brushed his shoulder, and Blake yelled after them, "Hey, watch where you're going, lame-brains! Knock-kneed ugly old losers."

Kitty Wheeling yelled back at Blake, "You're the

big loser, falling asleep in class."

"Yeah," laughed Molly O'Toole.

Blake trudged home, wolfed down his snack, and hurried up to his room. He was eager to write down the day's brilliant insults on the magic black paper. He filled several pages with all the things he remembered saying that day, and one by one they joined the other insults hovering above his bed. The light was so bright Blake had to squint a little, but still he went on writing with the magic pen. When he came to the end of the mean things he had said, he found the list he'd made earlier in the week and began to copy the insults from there onto the black pages.

He worked steadily until dinnertime, completely ignoring his homework. After dinner, Mrs. Branson sent him back upstairs to do his math. Blake noticed with some satisfaction that he did not need to turn on his desk light; the glowing insults lit the whole room quite brightly.

Mr. and Mrs. Branson came upstairs to see how Blake was getting on. There was a faint glow coming from the door of his room.

Mr. Branson chuckled. "Too bad this can't

continue. Think of the savings on our utility bill."

They went into Blake's room and found Blake squinting over his homework beneath a harsh white glow. The entire ceiling and part of the walls were covered with sheets of the ragged-edged black paper. There were even papers stuck to the windows and the closet door, nasty remarks shining from each one of them with a glaring light.

Blake looked pale and pasty under the harsh light. He was rubbing his temples and he looked sick and cross.

"Blake," said his mother, "are you all right? You look terrible!"

"I have a headache," Blake said.

"I'm not surprised," said his father. "It's bright enough in here to blind you!" He shook his head in disbelief. "I hope you'll be able to sleep with all these words lighting up the room, Blake."

Blake kissed his parents good night and crawled into bed. No matter how tightly he shut his eyes the glowing ceiling kept him awake. He couldn't fall asleep, and the longer he squinted up at the ceiling, the more the black raggedy pieces of paper seemed

to take on scary shapes. His brilliant words no longer seemed very funny. He scrunched way down in his bed, pulled his pillow over his eyes and fell asleep. He had nightmares that the pieces of paper were chasing him, shouting insults and sticking to his body.

The next morning Blake had dark circles under his eyes, and he was so tired from sleeping poorly with all the bright glowing light that he could barely eat his breakfast. He fell asleep in class three times. When Molly O'Toole poked him in the back to wake him up he started to call her a baboon, but the thought of adding one more glowing remark to the collection on his ceiling made him clamp his mouth shut.

After school he fell asleep on the couch, and he was still sleeping there when his father got home from work. Mr. Branson shook him gently to wake him for dinner. Blake let out a yell and sat up, crying out, "Don't let the raggedy papers get me, Dad!"

"Calm down, Blake, it's only a dream," said Mr. Branson. He rubbed Blake's back a little. "Sounds like a doozy. Want to tell me about it?"

Blake began to cry. "Please, Dad, my room scares me. It's so bright I can't sleep. I really, really don't like to read all those mean things on my ceiling. I'm afraid of all those black raggedy pieces of paper flying around. Do I have to keep writing down mean things?"

Mr. Branson laughed. "Only if you plan to keep saying them."

Blake shuddered. "No way, Dad. I don't know why I ever said them in the first place. They used to seem funny, but they don't anymore. I'm sorry I ever called anyone such awful things."

"In that case, let's see what we can do about that collcction of yours," said Mr. Branson. "You grab a garbage bag and I'll get the broom."

When they walked into Blake's room all the black raggedy pieces of paper had fallen to the floor. The white insults were only faintly glowing now, and some had completely disappeared.

As they stuffed the last pieces of paper into the garbage bags and Blake's father put the magic pen in his pocket to return to Mrs. Piggle-Wiggle, he said, "Hey, maybe you can invite Chuckie to spend the night tomorrow."

Blake smiled happily up at his father as they dragged the full garbage bags out into the hall. "Great idea, Dad!" he said. "Except . . . maybe the day *after* tomorrow. I've got a lot of sleep to catch up on!"

The Picky-Eater Cure

"Will Pemberton, you have been turning down your mouth and making faces at your plate for long enough!" Will's mother pleaded as she watched her son pick his way through yet another meal.

"Only one tiny piece of chicken has passed your disapproving lips since you sat down. You haven't eaten a single grain of that rice you've been pushing around your plate—or a bite of that salad you're hiding under your napkin."

"But, Moommm!" Will whined as he speared a lettuce leaf with his fork by mistake.

"Ack! ACK!" Will began waggling and waving his fork back and forth at arm's length, trying to dislodge the hated greens.

Whish! The lettuce leaf flew off the fork and landed—splat!—right in his father's water glass. Mr. Pemberton glared at his son as he fished the dripping lettuce out of the glass.

"That's enough nonsense for one evening, young man. Pick up your fork and eat your dinner NOW!"

Will squinched up his face, flared his nostrils, then clutched his throat and pretended to gag. "But there's *parsley* in this rice! You know I hate green stuff! And I *don't* like smelly chicken. It tastes gross. Blehhhh!" Will shivered exaggeratedly and pushed his plate away. "Why can't I just have plain white noodles like the Magill kids' mom makes for them? I love plain noodles—and they don't smell bad either."

With a sigh, Mr. Pemberton pushed back his chair, stood up, and swept Will's plate off the table. "That's it. I've had it! If you won't eat what your mother cooked for you, then you won't eat at all. Go to your room and get ready for bed, young man!"

Still muttering and complaining under his breath, Will moped up the stairs to his bedroom.

As Mr. and Mrs. Pemberton took their coffee and dessert into the living room, Mrs. Pemberton said to her husband, "Pete, don't you think we were a little unfair to poor Will? He could have an upset stomach. Or maybe the poor dear has a sore throat. I'll take him a cold glass of milk and a few cookies in a few minutes. I just hate the thought of our little boy going to bed on an empty stomach."

Mr. Pemberton sighed and shook his head, but said, "Whatever you think, dear."

When Mrs. Pemberton went upstairs with the snack she had fixed, she found Will sitting on the floor playing with his chemistry set, not getting ready for bed as he had been told. Will's face brightened for a moment at the sight of the treats. He eagerly reached for a cookie but recoiled almost immediately in disgust. He made a face at the plate of cookies, then looked up at his mother reproachfully.

"Yuck!" Will said with a frown. "Mother, those are *raisin* cookies. You *know* I hate raisins." He turned back to his chemistry set and continued looking at a grape very intently with his magnifying glass. "I'm sure there's a worm in here somewhere," he said as he peered at the grape.

"Will, would you please stop monkeying around and get ready for bed right NOW!" Mrs. Pemberton ordered.

"I was only working on this important project for Mrs. Piggle-Wiggle," he whined.

Will slowly packed up his chemistry set and got into bed.

The next morning Will came bouncing down to breakfast with a big smile on his face. "'Morning, Mom!" he said happily.

Mrs. Pemberton smiled. "Well, I'm glad to see you looking so bright and cheery this morning, dear! I must say, it's a nice change from last night—you must be feeling better. Did you sleep well, sweetheart?"

Will slid into his chair and patted his tummy. "I sure did. And, boy, am I starving! What's for breakfast?"

"Ah, music to my ears!" Mrs. Pemberton smiled. She brought over a steaming plate of pancakes and sausage and placed it in front of Will. Suddenly he stopped smiling, grabbed his nose, and began coughing.

"PEEEUUUUWW! What's that awful smell? Is that sausage? Ugh and double yuck! How disgusting!"

Too hungry to make his mother take the plate away to remove the offending sausages, Will grabbed for the syrup with one hand and began to pour it over his pancakes. With the other hand, he took his fork and began pushing the sausages gingerly to the far side of his plate. He was so focused on getting the sausage as far away from the pancakes as possible, that he forgot about the maple syrup pouring out of the pitcher. A pool of syrup began to spread across the plate, floating the pancakes closer and closer to the sausages.

"Aaghh!" Will noticed just in time and frantically began to poke at the pancakes, spinning them in little circles to avoid contact with the sausages. In doing so, he also spun some of the syrup right off his plate, leaving a sticky puddle on the table.

Will's father watched in silence as Will spun and picked at his pancakes, eating only a few bites. Will speared a strawberry on his fork and sniffed at it daintily, then peered at it with a sour look on his face. Instead of putting the berry in his mouth, he dropped it into the sea of syrup with a splashing *plop*.

"*Hmph!*" Will's father put down the morning paper and said in a stern voice, "Okay, son, that's enough nonsense this morning. Eat or you'll be late for school."

Will sighed loudly, turning the corner of his mouth down so far that his lips practically disappeared. He slowly ate three bites of a pancake. Then he picked up his glass, squeezed his eyes tightly shut, and drank half of his chocolate milk, just enough to wash down the taste of the pancakes.

Mrs. Pemberton sighed.

"Time for school," she said. She briskly removed Will's dishes and brought them to the sink, noticing how little Will had eaten of his breakfast. "I'm sure you'll be very hungry by lunchtime, dear."

Will's father just said, "All right, Picky Pemberton, get some of that syrup rinsed off and I'll give you a ride to school on my way to work."

When Will and his father left, Mrs. Pemberton sat down at the kitchen table and wondered how, in the space of just a few weeks, her little boy had changed from a hearty eater who devoured almost anything that was put in front of him, to this picky, finicky face-maker. Suddenly Mrs. Pemberton had an idea.

"I know just what to do! I'll make his favorite, a bacon and tomato sandwich. He'd never turn up his nose at that!" she said to herself with satisfaction.

When Will came bounding through the kitchen door at lunchtime, the sandwiches were waiting. His mother had even made brownies for dessert, in the hope that for once Will would eat without face-making, gagging, groaning and complaining about how much he didn't like the taste of this or the smell of that.

"Look, dear! It's your favorite!" Mrs. Pemberton said hopefully, as Will sat down at the table.

But Will just pulled the delicious sandwich apart

bit by bit. He leaned in and examined the bacon, sniffing in distaste. He scraped at the small specks of salt and pepper on the tomatoes.

Finally, Will picked up his napkin. Mrs. Pemberton held her breath in anticipation—finally, Will was going to eat! But then he proceeded to pick up the lettuce with the napkin, fold it, and put it on the table away from the plate. His mother let out her breath in a disappointed *whoosh*.

Will then began his customary poking and picking. "These tomatoes taste sour and yucky," he said, squinching up his face. "I don't understand why I can't just have plain white noodles! Mrs. Magill makes them all the time."

This was just too much for Mrs. Pemberton. "But I thought you loved bacon and tomato sandwiches. At least you did until two weeks ago," she said.

Will didn't hear her. He was too busy peering at the brownies. He picked one up, took a tiny bite and slowly began to chew. Suddenly he started gagging. "Ack! Blech! Walnuts!" he exclaimed in disgust, spitting the minuscule bite of brownie back onto his plate. One by one he removed the walnuts from the brownie until only a pile of crumbs remained.

Fed up, Will's mother jerked the food from under Will's sniffing gaze.

"Go to school NOW. You're going to be late."

Will slumped and looked sulky as he went out the door. His mother could hear him as he whined his way out the gate. "Noodles, just noodles. That's all I want. I don't know why I can't just have plain noodles."

That evening when dinner was served, Will's behavior was the worst his mother and father had seen so far.

"Ugh! What's that *horrible* smell?" Will said in disgust as he sat down at the dining room table. He pinched his nose dramatically and flung himself out of his chair. Not finished yet, he then began rolling around on the dining room floor, clutching his throat, sticking out his tongue, and making the most awful gagging sounds.

His mother said, "Will, that's enough. Get up off the floor, sit in your chair like a gentleman, and eat your dinner."

Will obeyed, but continued to make coughing noises under his breath while his mother brought the food to the table.

All through dinner, Will pretended to gag on each tiny flake of broiled salmon. He clutched his throat with each bite of potato. He poked and prodded at the fresh peas and carrots from his mother's garden until they were all in a pile on the far edge of his plate.

Mr. Pemberton watched this dramatic performance for about twenty minutes, then said in a very loud voice, "Young man, your rude treatment of this delicious food is an insult to your mother and all of her hard work, and I refuse to stand for it anymore. If you won't eat the meal your mother prepared, then you won't have any dinner at all. Go upstairs, brush your teeth, and go to bed."

With a put-upon sigh, Will pushed his chair back from the dinner table and trudged up the stairs. Mr. and Mrs. Pemberton could hear him as he noisily thumped and bumped his way up to his room, whining and complaining in a loud voice, "Fish, ugh! Old smelly fish, icky, stinky, slimy fish. I haaaaate fish. It tastes even a million times worse than it smells. And peeeeeaaasss 'n' carrots—double, triple yucka-hooey!" Will made a spitting noise and one final dramatic gag as he slammed the door to his room.

Mr. Pemberton got out of his chair and gave his wife a reassuring hug as she tearfully cleared the table. "Mildred, why don't you call some of our friends about Little Inspector Sniff-and-Poke. I'm sure we aren't the only parents to ever have a child who's a picky eater," he said.

"What a wonderful idea! I'll call MaryJo Wingstaff. Maybe she'll be able to help," Mrs. Pemberton said, her face brightening with hope. She bustled into the kitchen to call her neighbor.

Mrs. Wingstaff answered in a singsong voice after only two rings, "Hello, Wingstaff residence. Mrs. Wingstaff speaking."

Mrs. Pemberton said, "Oh MaryJo, I'm so glad you answered! I need some advice. We're having the most awful problems with Will. He's turned into a terrible picky eater in the last few weeks. He won't eat ANYTHING. He just keeps asking for plain white noodles."

"Oh my dear Mildred, how horrible for you. Hartwig and I have not had a single worry about picky eating, thank goodness. Ariel and Finch always eat every delicious thing I put in front of them. Of course, they do have their favorites—don't we all?—but every day they beg for my special peanut butter and pickled herring sandwiches on pumpernickel bread. And just tonight I made our favorite dinner—brussels sprout and anchovy quiche with a graham cracker crust. It disappeared like magic! Would you like the recipe? I know you would all love it."

Mrs. Pemberton could hardly keep from laughing as she said, "No, thank you, MaryJo. I wouldn't dream of taking one of your family's favorite recipes. But I appreciate the offer. I'll call you later." Mrs. Pemberton hung up the phone feeling a little sick to her stomach at the thought of the Wingstaffs' favorite foods.

"Well, that was no help at all," she said as she

described the conversation to her husband. "I'll probably have better luck if I call Carol Magill—all Will talks about are the noodles that the Magill kids get to eat all the time. Those five children can't *all* be picky eaters, even if Will does say they have noodles whenever they want."

Mrs. Pemberton called her friend, who answered the phone cheerfully. "Oh, Carol, I'm so glad you're still up. I was hoping you'd be able to help me out with Will, my picky eater. At every single meal these days he comes into the kitchen holding his nose, gagging, making faces, and saying 'Ugh! What's that smell?' And how your children get noodles whenever they want and why can't he have noodles, too."

Carol Magill laughed. "Oh yes, I know the old 'noodles, noodles, we'll only eat noodles' routine *very* well. I hate to admit it, Mildred, but I finally just started to give in to the complaints and cook noodles for almost every meal—with five picky eaters it's just easier. I've given up on making them eat normal foods. But why don't you call Mrs. Piggle-Wiggle? All the children in town love her. She seems to have magical cures that will fix anything.

I'll bet she has just the solution for you!"

When Mrs. Pemberton called Mrs. Piggle-Wiggle, she felt better just hearing her cheerful voice. "Hello, Mrs. Piggle-Wiggle, this is Mildred Pemberton. I believe you know my son, Will."

"Of course I do! Why, Will plays here almost every day with his friends," Mrs. Piggle-Wiggle said cheerfully. "Just the other day he brought a magnifying glass and helped me find the pesky worms that had been eating my geranium and getting into my raspberries. While he helped me in the garden he told me all about his chemistry set—he seems very interested in science."

"That makes me very happy to hear, Mrs. Piggle-Wiggle," said Mrs. Pemberton. "But in the past few weeks, Will has become the most terrible picky eater. He has turned every meal into a scientific exploration, picking apart each tiny morsel that I serve him. His reaction to everything that is put in front of him is just dreadful. He whines endlessly how all the other kids get noodles, especially the Magills, and why can't he have noodles all the time too," Mrs. Pemberton sighed. "I'm at my wits' end.

I don't know what to do. Do you have any advice?"

Mrs. Piggle-Wiggle laughed. "Ah yes, the nose-holding, pretend-retching, throat-clutching, how-awful-everything-smells-and tastes phase. I overhear the children discussing and acting this out a great deal. Definitely symptoms of the dread of every parent, Picky Eateritis. I have a cure that works just beautifully. Be sure and tell Will to stop here after school tomorrow and not to forget his magnifying glass and tweezers. He really is such a help with insect control, especially searching for the 'wreethy-writhy worms,' as he calls them, in my berry patch. Now don't worry, Mrs. Pemberton, the cure is quite dramatic, but it's also very simple, completely harmless, and you will all enjoy the results, especially Will. And best of all, it is guaranteed to work in just a few days!"

Mrs. Pemberton could hardly wait to tell Mr. Pemberton about her conversation with Mrs. Piggle-Wiggle.

The next morning, Will's mother cooked a wonderful breakfast of scrambled eggs, blueberry muffins, bowls of fresh raspberries with cream, and freshly squeezed orange juice. Will's father was thoroughly enjoying his meal—until he noticed that his son had a raspberry impaled on a toothpick. Will was staring at the raspberry with his magnifying glass and the tweezers from his chemistry set. Will removed each tiny hair and seed as he examined the center of the raspberry. "Blech! Seeds!" Will said as he made a face at the offending berry.

"William Pemberton—or shall I call you Picky Pemberton?—I don't care if an army of seeds are in your raspberries. Eat your breakfast!" Mr. Pemberton scolded in frustration.

Will still hadn't taken a bite; he was too busy making faces, stirring through his scrambled eggs in search of flecks of parsley and specks of pepper. He dismantled his muffin, picking out every single blueberry and leaving only a pile of muffin crumbs on his plate.

Mr. Pemberton had reached his limit. "Go to school, Will," he growled, snapping the morning paper.

"Will, dear," his mother said as she began to clear the table, "Mrs. Piggle-Wiggle wants you to stop by her house after school today to help her with something. She said not to forget to bring your magnifying glass and tweezers."

The front door was open when Will arrived. Mrs. Piggle-Wiggle called from inside, "Come in, Will. I'm so glad you're here! And how wonderful, you brought your magnifying glass and tweezers. I was hoping to pick my raspberries today. Now you can help me search out those pesky old wreethy-writhy worms. I certainly don't want them in my raspberry jam. But first let's have a nice piece of gingerbread."

Mrs. Piggle-Wiggle's pet pig, Lester, was sitting at the table daintily sipping a cup of tea. Will sat down next to him and watched with a stricken look as Mrs. Piggle-Wiggle began serving large pieces of the warm, fragrant gingerbread.

Mrs. Piggle-Wiggle smiled at Will. "What's wrong, dear? Don't you like gingerbread?"

Will hung his head and looked very embarrassed. "No, thank you. I really just like noodles," Will said, still staring at the plate Mrs. Piggle-Wiggle had put in front of him.

Mrs. Piggle-Wiggle opened the large cupboard

next to the stove, took out a glass jar with a shaker lid, and put it on the kitchen table. Will could see that the jar was filled with glowing rainbow-colored, snowflake-shaped crystals. Mrs. Piggle-Wiggle said with a twinkle in her eye, "Just shake a little of this on your gingerbread, Will."

Will picked up the glowing shaker and sprinkled a few of the colored crystals on the plate of ginger-bread in front of him. The crystals floated down, making a sizzling sound as they landed. Will stared in amazement as a swirling rainbow-colored cloud rose, hiding the entire plate of offensive gingerbread. Even the smell had magically vanished.

Mrs. Piggle-Wiggle said, "Now, blow on the cloud gently three times and say, 'Noodles, noodles, please appear.'" Will did as Mrs. Piggle-Wiggle advised. Immediately the cloud vanished, and there in front of Will was a steaming plate of white noo-dles.

Will gasped in surprise and delight, then picked up his fork and dug right in. "Wow, this is really, really cool, Mrs. Piggle-Wiggle! I love noodles!" Will exclaimed, his mouth full of mushy white noodles.

"Wish I could take some of this home to put on the yucky food my mom makes that I'm supposed to eat. I keep telling my folks that all I really like to eat are noodles, just plain white noodles, but they don't listen."

"Of course you may take the jar home with you, Will, dear," Mrs. Piggle-Wiggle said. "I'll put it in this pretty purple drawstring pouch with a note for your parents. Before we finish, would you mind sprinkling some crystals in Penelope's dish for me? She's not been too fond of her food lately either."

Will took the jar of rainbow crystals out of the velvet drawstring pouch and sprinkled some of the crystals on the parrot's dish. Penelope watched intently as the seeds began to sizzle and the small rainbow-colored cloud covered her food. Will blew on the cloud, made his magic command, and there in Penelope's dish instead of birdseed were noodles, lots of noodles. Penelope flapped her wings and repeated, "Noodles, noodles, all I want is noodles. Awwwkkkk!"

Lester, who was enjoying a second helping of gingerbread, carefully shielded his plate with a napkin as Will bounded back to the table with the jar of crystals. Wag put his paws over his dog biscuits and Lightfoot pushed her saucer of milk under Mrs. Piggle-Wiggle's chair to protect their meals from any stray crystals floating about, but Will didn't notice.

That evening when Mr. Pemberton came home, his wife showed him the jar of rainbow-colored crystals and read the note from Mrs. Piggle-Wiggle.

Dear Mr. and Mrs. Pemberton,

At each meal, and even on snacks, Will must sprinkle these crystals on his food. I showed him how the crystals work this afternoon. You will enjoy how fast this cure works! The crystals are harmless, the results are quite entertaining, and the jar magically never empties until Will is cured.

Mrs. Piggle-Wiggle

"Excellent!" Mr. Pemberton said as he handed the note back to his wife. "A little entertainment will be most welcome! I was getting tired of Picky Pemberton's usual mealtime antics. What smells so good, dear wife? I'm starving! I'm so hungry I could eat a horse!"

Mrs. Pemberton laughed at her husband's joke and said, "I've made what used to be one of our son's favorite dinners until a few weeks ago—spareribs and twice-baked potatoes. In fact, dinner is just about ready. Pete, would you call Will to the table? He's holed up in his room studying some of the worms he found at Mrs. Piggle-Wiggle's today."

When Will sat down at the table, he stared at his dinner, turned up his nose, swelled his nostrils, and made a ghastly face. "Ugh!" he groaned. "This stuff looks revolting! I could smell it all the way upstairs in my room."

At that moment, Will saw the jar of colored crystals his mother had put next to his plate. With a shout of delight—the first one his parents had heard him utter at the table in weeks—he picked up the jar and sprinkled the rainbow-colored snowflake crystals all over his plate, and even some in his milk. "Mom, Dad, you can eat those icky old spareribs, but *I'm* going to have plain white noodles, just like I wanted." The crystal flakes sizzled as they hit the ribs, and the small rainbow-colored cloud rose, hiding Will's entire dinner.

"Now watch this," Will said, carefully blowing three times on the hovering cloud and chanting, "Noodles, noodles, please appear." Will's parents stared in amazement as the rainbow-colored cloud vanished, leaving only plain white noodles on his plate and in his glass. Will said, "Oh boy, plain white noodles, yum! And even the terrible smell is gone!"

And he ate every last noodle on his plate.

The next morning, Will's mother cooked up waffles and bacon for breakfast. Out of habit, Will started to complain about the smell and make faces at his food. He shivered when his mother placed a small slice of melon on his plate. Then he remembered the jar of crystals, and without another word sprinkled his food, blew on the cloud, and commanded the noodles to appear. Once again, the small rainbow-colored cloud dissolved and there on Will's plate was a steaming mound of plain white noodles.

Within moments, Will's plate was empty, and

Will was rubbing his tummy in satisfaction. "Mmmmm!" he sighed. "I could eat this for breakfast every single day. I think I hear the Magills at the front gate. Just wait till I tell them about these magic crystals and how I can have plain white noodles anytime I want and don't have to eat any more gloppy old goop, just like them!"

When Will had gone off to school, Will's mother picked up the jar of rainbow crystals and held it up to the light. "This jar really is magic, Pete. The way Will has been sprinkling everything, you would think it would be empty by now. But it's just as full as when Mrs. Piggle-Wiggle sent it home."

Mr. Pemberton said, "Don't even think of spoiling my breakfast. Pass me some more bacon, Mildred. Plain white noodles? Ugh!"

Mrs. Pemberton laughed, and they both finished their breakfast.

When Will came home for lunch, he could smell the tuna fish sandwich his mother had made as soon as he walked through the door.

"Pee-eew! I haaate tuna fish—it's so stinky!" Will said. He held his nose with one hand and quickly poured the rainbow crystals with the other. He sprinkled the bowl of grapes, and of course the oatmeal-raisin cookies, and finally put a dash of crystals in his milk.

For the next few days at each meal, no matter what was served, Will sprinkled his food with the rainbow-colored crystals and turned everything into plain white noodles. Breakfast, lunch, dinner . . . he even sprinkled his after-school snacks. He turned an apple into noodles, a banana into noodles, a bag of potato chips into noodles, even a doughnut into noodles. And still the jar of crystals remained completely full.

On Friday evening, when Will's mother served the tossed green salad, he did roll his eyes and pretend to gag just a little, but didn't say a word as he picked up the jar of colored crystals and rather slowly and unenthusiastically sprinkled his spaghetti and meatballs. Halfway through his meal, he put down his fork.

"Is everything all right, Will?" his mother asked, her eyes dancing. "Eat up all your noodles! You wouldn't want to miss dessert—I've made an apple pie. Would you like me to go ahead and sprinkle some of your crystals on a slice?"

"Um, actually, Mom, I'm kinda full. May I please be excused to work on my worm project for Mrs. Piggle-Wiggle?" Will asked.

"Why of course you may, darling," Mrs. Pemberton replied, stifling a chuckle of delight.

After Will had left the room, his parents looked at each other and stared at the jar of rainbow-colored crystals. It was now only half full. Mrs. Pemberton said, "Pete, I think this cure just might be starting to work."

"Thank goodness!" Mr. Pemberton exclaimed in relief. "I know it's only been a few days, but if I have to see many more plates full of those mushy noodles, I'm going to lose *my* appetite!"

On Saturday morning, Will did not make a face or complain about the smell of the pancakes or bacon that were served to him. He made a rather quiet, halfhearted command of "Noodles, noodles, please appear," and began to slowly eat. A few times, Mr. Pemberton looked up from his own plate and noticed Will looking at the pancakes and bacon longingly, but he remained quiet, uttering only the occasional, "Mmmm, this bacon tastes wonderful—it's cooked just right!"

When Will had slowly slurped up the last noodle, his father said, "Let's go to the hardware store. We can stop at Papa Joe's Pizza Palace on our way home—I could go for a slice of extra-cheese with pepperoni on top! What do you say, sport?"

"Great idea, Dad," Will said as he grabbed his jacket and raced out the kitchen door. He didn't hear his mother call after him as he hopped down the back steps two at a time, "Will, you forgot your crystals."

"Don't worry, dear," Will's father said. "I think I detected a slight note of enthusiasm in our little Will's voice. I couldn't tell if it was the trip to the hardware store or the mention of Papa Joe's Pizza Palace. But just in case . . ." And he slipped the bag of magic crystals into his jacket pocket.

After they were through at the hardware store, Mr. Pemberton and Will made their way to Papa Joe's Pizza Palace. The minute they opened the door, they were met with a waft of warm, delicious, tomato-sauce-and-cheese-scented air floating out of the restaurant.

"Mmmm, the marvelous scent of freshly baked pizza!" Mr. Pemberton rubbed his hands together in delight and grinned at Will. "There's nothing like it, is there?"

Will smiled and started to answer his father, but Mr. Pemberton interrupted him, a serious look on his face.

"Oops, I'm sorry, son," he said. "Is the smell too much for you? I forgot that you don't like the smell of strong foods. We can go somewhere else, if you like."

Will took a moment, then replied in a quiet voice, "Uh, no . . . it's okay, Dad. Let's go in here."

Will and his father sat down at a table and began to read their menus. When Papa Joe himself came to take their order, they asked for the Papa Joe Special, a super-duper jumbo pizza pie with double extra cheese, pepperoni, and meatballs. After Papa Joe left their table, Will's father began rummaging around in his jacket pocket.

"Oh, I just remembered, Will—you forgot to

take your noodle crystals when we left the house, so I grabbed them for you. Wouldn't want you to have to eat pizza when you could be enjoying your plain white noodles—I know they're your favorite! Now, where could they . . . ah, got 'em!" With that, Mr. Pemberton placed the purple pouch containing the jar of crystals in the middle of the table with a loud *thump*. Everyone in the restaurant turned and looked at Will and his father, and at the jar of crystals sitting there.

At that moment, Papa Joe slapped a huge, steaming pizza, gooey with melted cheese, onto the table. Mr. Pemberton took a slice and placed it on a plate.

Will looked at the pizza. Then he looked at the jar of crystals. Finally, he looked straight at his father.

"You know, Dad, I think I'm kind of in the mood to give the pizza a try. To be honest, I'm kind of starting to get, well, a little tired of eating just those plain, mushy old white noodles. Can I please take this jar back to Mrs. Piggle-Wiggle? I'm sorry I've been such a picky eater. From now on, I'll eat whatever you and Mom want."

Mr. Pemberton grinned and passed a plate of pizza across the table to Will. "That sounds just fine, son. Why don't you go ahead and put the jar in your pocket? Then we can stop at Mrs. Piggle-Wiggle's on our way home to thank her and give back the crystals."

"Thanks, Dad!" Will grinned happily.

As he picked up the jar, Will got a funny look on his face. He gave the pouch a quick shake, then removed the jar and unscrewed the lid. He stared in disbelief. The jar was completely empty, and the shaker lid only glowed a tiny bit as he pulled the drawstring of the bag closed around it.

"Is something wrong, son?" Mr. Pemberton asked in concern. "You haven't changed your mind, have you? Would you rather have noodles after all?"

Will shoved the pouch into his pocket. "Nope! No more noodles for me!" he said, and took a big bite of the steaming, wonderful-smelling pizza.

FIVE

The Afraid-To-Try Cure

With a screech of his skateboard wheels, George O'Connor skidded to a halt in front of the Campbells' house, hopped off his board, and bounded up the front walk.

"Hi, Jonathan! What are you looking at? And what's the book about?" he said, tucking his skateboard under his arm. It was a beautiful day, and all up and down the street, children were running and jumping and playing on lawns and in driveways, happily shouting and laughing to each other. Except for Jonathan, who was crouched on the bottom step of his family's front porch, peering down at the cement walk, one of his how-to books lying open on the ground beside him.

Jonathan looked up. "Oh, hi, George. It's just some old ants. The book is about safe tree climbing. Mrs. Piggle-Wiggle said I could practice on her trees, so I was reading the book to learn all about the right way to climb a tree. But then I saw these ants. Boy, they're always in such a hurry!" he said, his face alight with curiosity.

Just then, George's brother Timmy came speeding along on his skateboard. He rolled right over the trail of tiny ants, then skidded to a stop.

"Watch out, Timmy!" Jonathan said. "You're squashing the ants."

"Aw, they're just ants!" Timmy scoffed. "Hey, I'll go get my magnifying glass. Then these dumb ants will really hurry as I roast them."

"Don't! They aren't doing anything to you," Jonathan said.

"Oh, forget the stupid ants, and forget the tree

climbing, Jonathan," George said. "I've got an even better idea. Let's go over to Mrs. Piggle-Wiggle's house. She said we could build a ramp in her driveway so we can practice jumps on our skateboards."

"Jumps?" Jonathan said with a worried look on his face. "I don't know about that. I've never done a jump before; I don't know how. Maybe I'll just watch. You know, so I can learn the right way to do it."

"Aw, Jonathan. Come on!" George coaxed. "You *never* want to try anything new—you always just want to watch. Skateboard jumps are fun, and they're not hard at all! I bet you can do one if you just try!"

"That's okay," Jonathan said. He hunched up his shoulders and looked down at the ground in embarrassment. "I don't mind watching for a while. I like to see how things are done first. Besides, I don't want to fall in front of everybody."

George just shook his head.

Jonathan's mother stepped out onto the porch. "Good morning, George. Good morning, Timmy. What are you boys up to today?"

"'Morning, Mrs. Campbell," the two O'Connor boys said in unison. "We're going over to Mrs. Piggle-Wiggle's house. She said we could build a ramp off her porch so we could practice skateboard jumps. Only Jonathan's afraid to try." They both laughed.

Mrs. Campbell looked at her son. Poor Jonathan looked more dejected than ever. She gave a small sigh. Starting recently, it seemed like Jonathan *never* wanted to try anything new. He had always been a cautious child, but now it was starting to get out of hand. For hours on end he would watch to see how things were done, what they were, and how they worked, without actually trying to do anything. But most of all, she knew, he was afraid to try because people might laugh at him if he didn't do well. "On the other hand," Mrs. Campbell thought, "maybe I should consider myself lucky that Jonathan *doesn't* want to try anything as reckless as skateboard jumps!"

"Boys, caution is not a fault to be made fun of," she scolded. "Jonathan isn't afraid, he just likes to see how things work before he tries anything new. Now run along, you three. Have fun, but be back in time for lunch. And for goodness' sake, be careful!"

The three boys skateboarded down the sidewalk to Mrs. Piggle-Wiggle's house. George and Timmy raced to see who could get there fastest. Jonathan lagged behind.

Back at the Campbell house, Jonathan's mother poured herself a cup of coffee. She sat down at the kitchen table and dialed her friend Carol Timbers. "Hi, Carol, this is Rochelle. I'm calling to invite Ricky and Woody to lunch today."

"That's very sweet of you, Rochelle. I'll send the boys over as soon as they get home from their mountain-climbing class. They're such adventurous little tykes! Why, just the other day I was telling Bentley about how the boys were practicing rappelling down the side of the house. We're both just so proud of our little shavers. It's such a shame that poor Jonathan is so timid. Of course, he is very kind, and so smart. But how difficult to have a child who is afraid to try new things."

"Thank you for your kind words, Carol, and for the heads-up about your little mountain climbers. I'll call you when it's time to pick up Ricky and

Woody." As she hung up the phone, Mrs. Campbell said to herself, "Well, I'm certainly going to watch those two like a hawk. Rappelling down the side of that old three-story house! How dangerous—for them *and* for the house!"

After lunch and a game of who can spit a watermelon seed the farthest, the boys decided to play basketball. At least Ricky, Woody, George, and Timmy wanted to play. Jonathan hunched up his shoulders and looked down at his feet.

"I don't know, you guys. It's pretty hot . . . and I'm barefoot . . . and I don't know the rules."

"Oh come on, Jonathan. We're all barefoot. And your mom said we could play in the sprinklers to cool off later. And the rules are easy. You just try to throw the ball through the hoop. You can learn as you play," Woody said as he tossed the basketball at him. "Catch, Jonathan!"

But instead of reaching out to catch the ball, Jonathan's hands remained frozen at his sides. The basketball hit him in the stomach, and Jonathan sat down with a thump on the lawn as the ball rolled past him. He looked down at his feet, embarrassed.

"Nah, that's okay. I'll just sit here and watch you guys play. Maybe I can learn if I just watch you for a bit."

A little while later, Mrs. Campbell walked out onto the porch with some lemonade and cookies for the boys. She was about to call out to them, when she noticed that Jonathan wasn't playing with the others. He was sitting off to the side, watching, an intent look on his face. She left the tray of snacks on the table quietly and went back inside.

That night, when Jonathan's dad got home from work, he said, "Hey son, let's test out that new basketball hoop we hung last weekend."

"I don't know, Dad. That hoop's so high, and I'm too short. Besides, I think the ball may be kinda big for me to hold."

"Jonathan, your mother told me your friends were here and wanted you to play basketball. Why didn't you at least give it a try, son?"

"I just can't, Dad. I get all nervous and my fingers get fumbly and I was afraid that everyone would laugh at me if I didn't do it right. So I just watched. I'm sorry, Dad."

Jonathan hung his head and hunched his shoulders as he sadly stared down at his feet.

"Jonathan," his dad said, "not everyone has to be good at things before they try. In fact, the way to get good at something is by practicing it over and over. Come on, let's go practice!"

Jonathan thanked his father again, but shook his head. "No thanks, Dad. I think I'll just go upstairs and read for a while."

That evening before bed, Jonathan and his mother read a chapter of *The Jungle Book* together. When they finished, Mrs. Campbell bent down to kiss Jonathan good night. Jonathan looked up at her.

"You know what I want to be when I grow up, Mom? A veterinarian, so I can help animals like that doctor that we saw on TV. What was his name?"

"James Herriot, dear. If you like, I'll read some of his books to you. Sleep well, son. Your dad and I are very proud of you."

When Jonathan's mother went downstairs, she said to Jonathan's father, "Guess what Jonathan said he wanted to be when he grows up?"

"Certainly not a pro basketball player, I'm sure of

that," Jonathan's father said. "Or a professional skateboarder, for that matter."

"No, Robert. Jonathan said that he wants to be a veterinarian. He has such a love for animals. I think we should consider getting him a dog of his own. The O'Connor's poor old dog, Suzie, spends more time here with Jonathan than she does with the O'Connors. Let's think about it, can we?"

The next morning after breakfast, Jonathan's mother asked him if he was going to play baseball with his friends. Jonathan said, "I don't think so, that bat is too heavy for me to swing. And I never can catch the ball without dropping it. Could we go to the pet store instead and get some treats for Suzie and Mrs. Piggle-Wiggle's pets?"

"That's a lovely idea, Jonathan. Of course we can."

When Jonathan and his mother came home from shopping, Suzie was waiting on the front porch with George and Timmy.

"Hey, Jonathan, we won our baseball game today since you weren't there to drop the ball. Guess you'd rather play with our old dog than with us," George chuckled.

Jonathan knelt down and gave Suzie a hug, burying his face in her warm fur so that George and Timmy wouldn't see his hurt expression. "Good girl, wait till you see what I got for you today at the pet store." Suzie wagged her tail and eagerly licked Jonathan's cheek. Jonathan giggled with delight.

Inside, Jonathan's mother was putting away the groceries. Just as she placed the last can of creamed corn in the cupboard, the phone rang. She was surprised to hear Mrs. Piggle-Wiggle's voice on the line.

"I'm sorry to bother you, Mrs. Campbell, but I was hoping that Jonathan could help me this afternoon. If it's all right with you, of course? I can't give Lester or Wag a bath without his help. He has such a gift with my animals."

"Of course, Mrs. Piggle-Wiggle. I'm sure Jonathan will be delighted to help you. In fact, he bought some special treats for Lester and Wag at the pet store today. I'll send him right over. Maybe your pets will cheer him up. He's been feeling rather left out lately. Some of the boys have been teasing and bullying him about his lack of trying when it comes to sports."

"Yes, I did notice that," Mrs. Piggle-Wiggle said. "He's been wanting to climb that tree of mine for ages, I know, but keeps reading books on the subject and watching the other children, because he thinks it will make him more prepared. You know, Jonathan's desire to understand how things are done before he tries them is a sign of wisdom. But at the same time, sometimes the best way to learn how to do something is to just try it. Let me think about it for a bit. I'm sure my animals and I will be able to help."

"Thank you, Mrs. Piggle-Wiggle," Mrs. Campbell said gratefully as she watched Jonathan brushing Suzie.

After lunch, Jonathan carefully packed the treats for Mrs. Piggle-Wiggle's animals in his backpack. Suzie was fast asleep in the makeshift dog bed—really a pile of soft old towels—that he had fixed for her by the back door. Jonathan smiled when he saw Suzie's head resting on a squeaky dog toy. Her paw covered one of the special dog treats that he had bought for her, protecting it from theft.

"Have fun, dear. Be home in time for dinner,"

Mrs. Campbell said, giving her son a big hug.

When Jonathan got to Mrs. Piggle-Wiggle's house he noticed with relief that the usual taunting, teasing, whooping, and hollering boys were not there, and that the skateboard jump had been moved from the porch steps.

Lester, Mrs. Piggle-Wiggle's pet pig, was sunning himself lazily on the top step. Wag came running to greet him, and Lightfoot the cat bounded not far behind. From her perch on the porch, Penelope the parrot called eagerly, "Hello, hello!" And Mrs. Piggle-Wiggle's pony, Spotty, whinnied happily as Mrs. Piggle-Wiggle herself led him around the side of the house.

"My goodness, Jonathan, what a greeting you always get from my animals! I'm so happy that you were able to help me today. There are so many times that I don't know what I would do without your expertise."

Jonathan carefully put his backpack down on the porch steps.

"Wait till you see the treats I've brought for all of you today!" he said to the animals. "And we didn't forget you, either, Mrs. Piggle-Wiggle! Mom sent you a jar of her special raspberry-strawberry-blackberry jelly. She made it yesterday," Jonathan said, proudly handing her the jar of ruby-red jelly.

"Wag, I brought you a bag of special dog biscuits. Here's a jar of cat treats for Lightfoot. Lester, some of your favorite apples. For you, Penelope, I got grapes. And Spotty, here's a big bunch of carrots just for you," Jonathan said as he emptied the treats from his backpack.

Together, Jonathan and Mrs. Piggle-Wiggle distributed the treats. Jonathan gave Penelope six grapes from the large bunch. Lester carefully cut one of his apples up, politely offering a slice to Jonathan. Wag sat up to beg for a dog biscuit, wagging his tail so hard that he tipped over. Lightfoot purred loudly when Jonathan gave her a handful of the cat treats in her dish. And Spotty, waiting patiently by the porch steps, got two of the fresh crunchy carrots. Mrs. Piggle-Wiggle and Jonathan put the remaining treats in the kitchen.

"Now, while they enjoy their treats, why don't you and I have a glass of lemonade to cool us off before we tackle bathing Wag and Lester," Mrs. Piggle-Wiggle said. "I've put all the towels, brushes, soap, and the big washtub out under the tree in the backyard. And the hose reaches the washtub perfectly, so we can rinse Wag and Lester with warm water. I'm sure Spotty will want a bath too." Mrs. Piggle-Wiggle and Jonathan laughed when they saw Spotty nodding his head.

"And I have some old T-shirts in the house that you can wear. We don't want you to get your nice clothes soaking wet, do we?" asked Mrs. Piggle-Wiggle.

"It's okay," Jonathan smiled. "I brought a change of clothes in my backpack. Besides, I don't care if I get wet. I love giving your pets baths!"

Mrs. Piggle-Wiggle said, "You're such a help! I can hold them still if I have to, but I have trouble getting down on my hands and knees. You are so much more agile than I am, Jonathan, and Wag and Spotty never seem to move at all when you take care of them. You definitely have a gift when it comes to animals."

Soon all the animals were bathed, brushed, and

dried off. Jonathan even cleaned and polished Spotty's hooves. Then he helped Mrs. Piggle-Wiggle put away the washtub and coiled the hose for her. Mrs. Piggle-Wiggle washed the towels, and Jonathan was just hanging them up to dry when George, Timmy, Ricky, Woody, Sean, and Blake came skateboarding down the sidewalk, shouting and shoving each other playfully. They turned onto the walk.

"Let's fix up the skateboard jump," Woody said as he banged into the front step of Mrs. Piggle-Wiggle's porch.

"Boys," Mrs. Piggle-Wiggle said, "I would rather you kept the jump on the side of the house."

"Sure thing, Mrs. Piggle-Wiggle," Blake said.

"Wow, Jonathan, you missed a super ball game. Here, catch!" Ricky Timbers said as he threw Wag's tennis ball at Jonathan. Wag jumped up in the air, caught the ball in his mouth, then went over to Jonathan, who was sitting on the bottom porch step, and dropped it at Jonathan's feet.

"I guess you want me to play with you, huh, Wag?" Jonathan said. "But I'm no good at throwing a ball."

By now the other boys were jumping, twisting, and crashing on their skateboards. They forgot all about teasing Jonathan as they double-dog-dared each other into more jumps and spins. Jonathan stood and watched silently, as Lightfoot rubbed up against his leg.

Just then, Woody Timbers came roaring up to Jonathan on his skateboard close to Lightfoot's tail. Lightfoot tensed in surprise, then let out an awful yowl and raced around the house, climbing the big tree in the backyard like double-greased lightning. She scampered up the trunk and cowered on a branch near the top, shivering.

"Oh, dear!" Mrs. Piggle-Wiggle said. "I don't think I'll ever be able to coax her down."

The boys had all stopped what they were doing and gathered around the trunk of the tree with Mrs. Piggle-Wiggle.

"I'm sorry, Mrs.Piggle-Wiggle. I didn't see her," Woody said, blinking back the tears that were welling up in his eyes.

Jonathan came running down the porch steps two at a time, calling to Mrs. Piggle-Wiggle as he ran toward the group gathered around the tree.

"Don't worry, Mrs. Piggle-Wiggle. I called the fire department; they rescue animals all the time. They're bringing a big ladder, and I've been studying the tree for weeks to see which are the strongest branches to climb on, so I can tell them the best way up."

When the fire truck pulled up, Jonathan ran out to meet it.

"You must be the young man in charge here, Jonathan Campbell. Am I right?" the first fireman said. He winked at the other fireman as the two of them carried the ladder into the yard.

"I'm so glad that Jonathan called you," Mrs. Piggle-Wiggle said. "Poor Lightfoot is afraid of heights, and I don't think she'll ever come down on her own. Someone will have to climb up to get her."

The two firemen put the tall extension ladder up against the tree. One of the firemen held the ladder steady, while the other began to slowly climb upward. However, before the fireman even got halfway up, Lightfoot mewed in fright and moved even further out on the branch.

The fireman slowly climbed back down the ladder to the ground.

"I'm sorry, Mrs. Piggle-Wiggle," he said. "Lightfoot just won't let me get anywhere near her. And now she's so far up in the tree, where the branches aren't as thick. I don't think they'll hold my weight."

"Oh, dear," said Mrs. Piggle-Wiggle in dismay.

Jonathan stepped toward Mrs. Piggle-Wiggle and the firefighters. "Lightfoot trusts me, Mrs. Piggle-Wiggle. I can climb up and bring her down," he said with a serious look on his face.

When they heard that, the group of boys just stood with their mouths open.

Mrs. Piggle-Wiggle said, "It's true. If anyone can get Lightfoot down, it's Jonathan. He has a wonderful way with her, and all of my pets. And he knows everything there is to know about tree climbing."

The fireman holding the ladder smiled down at Jonathan and said, "We climb as a team, son. My partner will follow you up the ladder. You're the man in charge here. We'll follow your lead."

Jonathan, his backpack hanging from his

shoulders, climbed carefully up the ladder with the fireman right behind him. The growing group of children didn't make a sound as they watched Jonathan hop onto a branch. With both hands firmly grasping the branches nearest him, Jonathan scrambled up through the branches and eased his way toward Lightfoot as slowly and carefully as possible, so he wouldn't startle her. Lightfoot meowed pitifully.

"Don't worry, Lightfoot," Jonathan said in a soft, gentle voice. "I've come to rescue you. I'm going to put you right into my backpack and carry you back down to Mrs. Piggle-Wiggle. You always like riding around in my backpack, don't you? You'll be safe, I promise. Just stay still while I pick you up."

Jonathan carefully and very gently eased the terrified Lightfoot into his backpack and swiftly closed the flap most of the way. Jonathan had read somewhere that cats who are being transported in carriers feel safer in the dark. Lightfoot didn't meow or struggle. Jonathan followed the fireman down the ladder, murmuring softly and soothingly to Lightfoot the whole way.

Finally, Jonathan's feet touched the ground, and the crowd of children let up a cheer. Jonathan held a finger to his lips to quiet the children, then gently took Lightfoot out of his backpack and handed her to a beaming Mrs. Piggle-Wiggle. He never saw Lightfoot wink at Mrs. Piggle-Wiggle nor heard Mrs. Piggle-Wiggle whisper "Thank you" to her cat while she rubbed its ears.

"Jonathan, that was a brave deed you did just now. I can't begin to tell you how grateful I am and how proud I am of you. No one will think you are afraid to try anything ever again," Mrs. Piggle-Wiggle said.

"Hooray for Jonathan, champion tree-climber!" George O'Connor shouted. "Hooray for Jonathan!" the other children echoed.

"Wow, Jonathan," Blake said. "I've never seen anyone ever climb Mrs. Piggle-Wiggle's big old tree so fast. Could you maybe teach me how to do it?"

"Sure!" said Jonathan. "It's real easy. Mainly, I just watched other people climb, to see which branches were strongest, and which way was the fastest path to the top."

"And how did you know you should put Lightfoot into the backpack?" Woody asked. "That was so cool!"

"Well, I read about it in a book once," Jonathan answered. "But I wasn't sure it would work until I tried it!"

At these words, George O'Connor started to laugh. The other children soon joined in. Jonathan looked confused for a moment, but when he realized what he had said, he grinned a little sheepishly, then started to laugh as well, as the other children once again began to pat his back and congratulate him on a job well done.

The two firemen smiled at Jonathan and each shook his hand. The first fireman said, smiling down at Jonathan, "We could use more brave boys like you. Cats are the hardest animals for us to rescue."

The second fireman patted Jonathan on the back and said, "Thank you for helping us today, Jonathan. How would you like a ride home on the fire engine?"

"Are you serious?" Jonathan exclaimed. "That would be *great*!"

And wearing an honorary fireman's hat, Jonathan the hero rode proudly between the two firemen, with a trail of cheering skateboarders following him all the way home.

SIX

The Messy Stuff-
and-Cram Cure

"**G**ood morning, sleepyhead! Breakfast is—"

Mrs. McCloud's words choked off mid-sentence when she opened Katy's bedroom door. The neatly folded laundry she had placed on Katy's bed the night before now lay in a jumbled pile on the floor.

"Katy McCloud! I told you to put away those clothes last night!" Mrs. McCloud threw up her hands in exasperation. "Why do you have to be so messy?"

Katy mumbled an apology and got out of bed. Mrs. McCloud just shook her head and went downstairs. Katy began rummaging through the pile of clothes. She found a pair of clean jeans and a wrinkled shirt, which she was pretty sure was clean but turned out to be the one she had worn on Saturday when she helped Mrs. Piggle-Wiggle weed her flower bed. Katy tossed the dirty shirt back onto the floor and hunted around for a clean one. She opened a dresser drawer, pawed through it, and finally yanked it all the way out and dumped the contents on the bed. Among the crumpled shirts and blouses were a number of stray socks, some pajama bottoms, several scraps of paper, a few crumpled candy wrappers, a bent soda straw, and a stuffed teddy bear with one eye missing. At the very bottom of the pile she found a shirt that looked reasonably fresh. She dug clean socks out of the jumble of laundry on the floor, managing to shove half the clothes under her bed in the process. She then poked around in her closet in search of her tennis shoes, eventually finding one in her wastebasket and one under her desk.

"Katy, hurry!" called her mother. "You'll be late for school!"

Katy rushed into the bathroom, where she had to fish her hairbrush out of the laundry hamper. (This was made somewhat easier, of course, by the fact that all her dirty clothes were scattered across her room rather than placed inside the hamper.) She brushed her hair, brushed her teeth, and washed her face, tossing the damp face cloth into the sink before skittering downstairs for breakfast.

When Katy's mother walked into the bathroom, she almost tripped over the wet towels on the floor. The drawer was hanging open, and inside was a capless tube of toothpaste squeezed in the middle, oozing onto a moldy apple core, a half-eaten sandwich, and an assortment of colored pencils. A hairbrush full of Katy's curly hair was resting on the edge of the counter, along with orange peelings, wads of paper, an old sock, a doll's wig, and an empty soda pop can.

Katy's mother shook her head and sighed. "The minute Katy gets home this afternoon she *has* to clean up this mess."

When Katy arrived at school, she hurried to her

locker to find the notebook she was supposed to turn in yesterday. "It must be in here somewhere," Katy said as she took off her backpack, tossing it at the foot of her locker so she could put her lunch and jacket away. The locker door seemed to be stuck shut. Katy tugged and pulled on the handle but it wouldn't open. Then she put her foot and shoulder against the door and yanked really hard. She didn't notice the dangling sweater sleeve or the gym sock that were obviously jamming the locker door. After much tugging, banging, kicking, and pulling, the locker door finally flew open, knocking Katy onto the hall floor. Everything that she had hurriedly been stuffing and cramming inside the locker for weeks came tumbling out. Pens, pencils, crumpled papers, and several old wadded-up lunch bags went rolling down the hall, followed by two half-eaten apples and a moldy orange. The missing notebook, along with overdue library books, a baseball cap, and a tennis shoe now lay in a large heap at Katy's feet. She began kicking the big mess aside as she frantically searched for the notebook. Katy was sitting cross-legged on top of her backpack when she looked up and saw her teacher Mrs. Rosemont glaring down at her.

"Katy, what in the world is all this racket? What an awful mess. Hurry and pick this up or you'll be late for class. I'm afraid you will have to remain after school today so you can organize your locker. I'll write your mother a note and tell her why I'm keeping you and also why I'm giving you a bad grade for the day."

"I'm sorry, Mrs. Rosemont. I'll hurry," Katy said as she pawed through the heap on the floor, finally finding the notebook she needed for class. When she picked up her backpack she noticed that she hadn't closed it and her homework was sticking out. Katy shrugged, then scooped and shoved the big mess back into her locker. She punched her jacket into a wad so it would fit, jammed her lunch bag on top, slammed the locker door shut, and hurried down the hall to class with her backpack shedding loose papers behind her the entire way.

That afternoon when Katy came trudging home from school, her mother was in the kitchen putting away groceries.

"My goodness, Katy, you're late today," Mrs. McCloud said with a worried look on her face.

"I know, Mom, I'm sorry." Katy hung her head as she handed Mrs. Rosemont's note to her mother.

Katy's mother couldn't hide the disappointment she felt as she read the note from Katy's teacher.

Dear Mrs. McCloud,

I had to keep Katy after school today to straighten up her locker. Katy is smart and extremely willing to please, but so messy and disorganized that I am afraid her grades will suffer because of this.

Sincerely,
Grace Rosemont

When Katy's mother put the note on the kitchen table, she almost fell when she stumbled over the backpack that Katy had tossed on the floor.

"Katy, I can't begin to tell you how disappointed I am. This endless messiness of yours is not just causing problems at home, but now at school. Go to your room and pick up the mess you left this morning. And don't forget your homework. Now march, young lady, and take your backpack with you. I'll call you when dinner is ready."

Katy hurried up to her room, dumped the contents of her backpack onto her unmade bed, swept everything off her desk onto the floor, grabbed a notebook out of the jumbled heap, and sat down to do her homework. She couldn't find a pencil, so she stirred through the pile on the floor with her foot. Then, Katy jerked hard on the top desk drawer. It wouldn't open, so she yanked on the next, and the next one after that, until she reached the bottom drawer. They were all jammed shut. In desperation, Katy dumped the contents of her wastebasket on her bed, where she finally found a pen—with no cap. She sat back down at the desk and began to do her homework, completely forgetting to pick up her room, which was now even messier than it had been when she got home just minutes before.

The next morning after Katy had left for school, once again trailing loose papers from her backpack, her mother walked slowly upstairs to Katy's room.

She stood in the doorway, feeling rather weak in the knees. The room was a disaster. There were clothes all over the floor, draped on the desk chair, hanging off the doorknob, tossed over the closet door, and peeking out from under the bed. Books lay in lopsided stacks on the floor, desktop, and windowsills—everywhere except in the bookcase. Heaps of clothes were on the unmade bed, a sock dangled over the desk lamp, and several clothes hangers hung on the curtain rod.

"Oh dear," sighed Katy's mother. She looked at her daughter's desk. Some of the drawers were partly open, crammed so that they couldn't be properly closed. In the top middle drawer, Mrs. McCloud found the pinking shears that she had been looking for all week. The shears had been used to cut up bits of colored paper that had obviously been wiped off the desk into the drawer in a jumble of paper clips, old rubber bands, broken crayons, chewing gum wrappers, part of a half-eaten sandwich, some doll clothes, two empty raisin boxes, crumpled wads of paper, and a pair of sunglasses with one lens missing.

Mrs. McCloud sat down on the edge of Katy's

unmade bed. "I guess I could spend all day cleaning up in here like I did last week, but what earthly good would it do?" she said to herself. "Katy will just come home and in a few hours the mess will begin again."

She gathered what laundry she could find, shut the closet door, and closed the half-open drawers as best she could. Then she went downstairs to the kitchen. She made a fresh pot of tea and called her friend Pamela Peasley.

"Pamela, I'm at my wits' end. Katy is such a slob, I can't stand it."

Mrs. Peasley laughed and said, "Oh, what a shame. My Prunella and Quinton are the MOST organized children. Why, sometimes Maxfield and I have to beg them to stop cleaning their rooms! Just the other day dear little Prunella lined all my kitchen drawers and Quinton cleaned the cupboards."

"Isn't that nice?" said Mrs. McCloud rather crossly, and she got off the phone as fast as she could. Suddenly she remembered how messy her sister Janet had been as a child. Janet was now the mother of three children and lived in a nice, tidy house.

Eagerly she dialed Janet's number and poured out her problem.

Janet laughed. "Sounds like Katy takes after her Aunt Janet! Remember how crazy I used to drive you? You were always neat as a pin. I'll never forget the time you told Mom my bed had so much junk under it that it was tipping sideways."

Mrs. McCloud couldn't help but chuckle. "But you aren't like that now," she said. "What happened?"

"I grew up," said Janet. "I'm sure Katy will grow out of her messiness *eventually*."

"I'm not sure I can wait that long!"

"Then maybe you should call Mrs. Piggle-Wiggle," suggested Janet. "She always seems to know how to break a bad habit."

"Of course!" said Mrs. McCloud. "Why didn't I think of that myself?"

She hung up and called Mrs. Piggle-Wiggle right away.

"Why, Mrs. McCloud! How lovely to hear from you. I so enjoy my visits from your little Katy. Such a bright, energetic child."

"Yes, but I'm afraid she's rather untidy," said Mrs. McCloud. "It would take a bulldozer to clean her room. Her dresser drawers are bursting at the seams!"

"Oh, she's a stuffer-and-crammer, is she? That's quite common among children her age, you know. And fortunately, the cure is very simple. I have some wonderful invisible paint that ought to do the trick."

"Invisible paint, did you say?" asked Mrs. McCloud doubtfully.

"Yes, indeed. You paint her dresser with it, her desk drawers, shelves, ledges, windowsills, and any other hidey holes in Katy's room and bathroom where she stuffs and crams. The paint doesn't show, because it's invisible, dries instantly, and there is no odor whatsoever. I'm sure you'll see that the results are rapid and quite dramatic. And"—Mrs. Piggle-Wiggle laughed—"I must add, a little noisy after the paint is applied. Now make sure to place just a dab on everything, even her bed and bedding, tops of doors, doorknobs, and especially her drawers, cupboards, and her closet. I'll have Hubert Prentiss bring the paint by this afternoon. I've invited Katy, Molly O'Toole, and Janie Beaumont over for tea after school today to help make plans for my birthday party in two weeks. All the children in town are invited, and the girls are especially excited to start decorating."

"Oh, Mrs. Piggle-Wiggle, how lovely! Yes, I've heard the girls talking and making all sorts of plans. I hear it's going to be a costume party. Now please, let me know if there is anything I can do to help. I'm sure a lot of the other mothers will want to contribute also."

"Thank you, Mrs. McCloud, but I think the children have the party plans well organized. I like to have them feel this is their party also, not just a celebration for me. Now before I forget, back to Katy's room. The girls will be here several hours, which should give you plenty of time to paint everything in Katy's room and bathroom. Ignore the racket in her room. It will subside quickly. And after you finish the paint dabbing and have shut the door to Katy's room, I suggest a calming cup of tea." Mrs. Piggle-Wiggle laughed.

After lunch, Katy's mother took the small can of invisible paint and the little brush up to Katy's room. She had just finished dabbing a tiny bit of paint on Katy's dresser and each drawer and had turned to begin on the desk when she heard what sounded like the drawers sliding open. She quickly turned and looked at the dresser. Each drawer had opened and the contents were flying out, landing on the floor. The top of the dresser was empty, with all Katy's mess swept off onto the floor.

"I'll have to hurry with all this paint dabbing or I won't be able to get out of the room," Katy's mother said, laughing. By the time Mrs. McCloud had finished and had shut the door to Katy's room and bathroom, the noise was deafening. "Mrs. Piggle-Wiggle was right, I do need a calming cup of tea."

That afternoon when Katy came home from Mrs. Piggle-Wiggle's house, she was bursting with excitement about the plans for the party.

After dinner, she hurried up to her room to start making decorations. When she opened the door to her room, she stared wide-eyed at the enormous mess. All the drawers had emptied themselves onto the floor. The closet door stood agape, revealing empty hangers. The hodgepodge of clothes now lay in mountainous heaps in the center of the room. The desk drawers had regurgitated their mishmash of contents and the desktop was swept clean. Everything that Katy had been cramming under her bed for weeks was cast out, joining the bedding on the floor. The bookshelves had purged themselves of Katy's muddled disorder. Not a single surface, drawer, or cupboard held any of Katy's endless stuffing and cramming. As she shoved and pushed her way into her room—of course, not picking anything up—she stepped on a half-filled box of cereal and tripped over a pile of bedding, landing hard on the floor. She finally made her way to her desk to work on paper-chain decorations for the party. Katy tried to sit down at her desk but the desk chair dumped her onto the floor with a thud. She tried again. *Thud!* After the third time she gave up and just sat on the floor. She stirred through the mess, searching for some colored paper.

Stumbling into the bathroom, Katy splashed water on her hands and face. She dried off with a used towel she found under her feet, then tossed it at the sink. Turning toward the door, the wet towel sailed through the air, swatting Katy on the back. *Thwap!*

Shoving and pushing her way across the room toward her bed, Katy tried kicking one of the large piles of clothing aside, only to have the clothes push *her* aside. One of her shoes even kicked her back.

"Ouch! Mean old stuff!"

Katy picked up a pile of clothes and threw them at the closet door. The clothes came flying back and landed with a hard slap, shoving Katy backward and onto the floor.

"I'll fix you!" Katy said.

She gathered up another one of the enormous piles and crammed it into one of the empty dresser drawers. *Whoosh!* The clothes came flying out, landing at her feet.

Katy began stuffing a pile of books, games, dolls, stuffed animals, more clothes, shoes, old crumpled bits of paper, gum wrappers, and an empty cereal box under her bed. *Zing!* It all shot right out the other side.

She picked up a stack of books and more papers and tossed them angrily on a shelf in the bookcase. *Plop!* Back onto the floor.

Next, Katy kicked one of the huge piles into her closet. She tried to force the door shut, but it swung wide and the pile came spilling right back out again.

"THIS IS NO FUN AT ALL!" Katy said crossly, and sat down on her desk chair. The chair immediately tipped her off onto the floor.

"That's it! I'm going to bed," Katy said as she looked hopelessly at the huge mess.

She grabbed her pillow off the floor and tossed it on the bed. *Whap!* The pillow soared into the air, hitting her in the face.

"Now what? I'm too tired for a pillow fight tonight." Katy sighed.

She began gathering up her bedding and her quilt and threw them onto the bed. Immediately the bedding slid off onto the carpet. Over and over, at least a dozen times, Katy threw the heap of bedding at her bed, only to have it fall repeatedly onto the floor.

"Okay, I give up, you mean old bed. See if I care. I'll sleep on the floor."

Katy made a nest out of the bedding, plopping it on top of a pile of belongings, and fell fast asleep on the floor.

Katy's mother and father looked in to see how their daughter was coping. They smiled when they saw Katy asleep on the huge pile she had created. She had pulled the quilt up to her chin, her pillow resting on top of a pile of books. A teddy bear and a bedroom slipper peeked out from the rumpled tangle.

All that night Katy had terrible dreams that her room had suddenly come to life. She dreamed that her clothes and all her belongings were swirling and dipping, as if they were dancing around the room. Each twirling mass seemed to be lit by an eerie assortment of changing colored lights. The sleeves and pant legs of her clothes took on ghostlike shapes that spookily seemed to be pointing at her as they flapped by. She dreamed she heard a chorus of voices whispering, *pick up, pick up, pick up, pick up, pick up*.

In her dream, the drawers of her dresser and desk slid open and shut by themselves. The cupboard doors in her room and bathroom rattled angrily. The closet door began to creak open and groan loudly as it shut itself over and over and over. All Katy's dolls and stuffed animals had lined up in a row on her desk and were glaring at her, whispering and pointing with hands and paws, *pick up, pick up, pick up, pick up, pick up.*

Katy dreamt she saw her bedroom window open wide. She watched in terror as all her clothes and belongings shoved and pushed their way into a huge mass and flew out the window. She watched sadly as everything vanished into the dark night sky.

Katy woke herself up when she shouted in her sleep, "No, no, wait! Please wait! Don't fly away."

She sat up in her makeshift tangle of bedding, scrubbing at her eyes as she looked around her room. The sun came streaming in through the windows, and Katy saw to her relief that nothing in her room had changed since the night before. All of her things were still there. It had all been just a bad dream.

As Katy stumbled her sleepy way into the bathroom, she heard her mother calling, "Katy, breakfast!"

Now wide-awake, Katy hurriedly searched for her hairbrush in the pile of dirty clothes, damp towels, and the collection of debris that had flung itself onto the bathroom floor.

"Aha! There you are." Katy grabbed her hairbrush as she kicked at the pile. Then she spied her toothbrush as she kicked aside another pile, stepping on the squashed—and open—tube of toothpaste oozing out next to the sink.

After Katy finished brushing her hair and her teeth, she washed her face and hands and dried off with a towel from the messy pile on the floor. She picked everything up and tossed it into the bathtub. This time Katy ducked her head as everything came flying back out at her.

As she stood in the doorway of her bedroom, she put her hands on her hips and stared defiantly back at her room.

"Okay, room, you win! Right after breakfast I'll pick up, pick up, pick up, pick up, pick up. I can't find a thing and I'm tired of living in this big mess and sleeping on the floor."

After breakfast, Katy went back to her room, armed with cleaning supplies and trash bags. Katy looked first at her bed. "If I make you neat as a pin, maybe you'll behave yourself." Katy swept a path to her bed and took off all the crusty, messy bedding. She got clean sheets out of the linen closet, pulled all the trash and clothes out from under the bed, organized her desk, bookshelves, and all of her drawers, carefully cleaned her closet, hung up her clothes in perfect order, lined up her shoes, and gathered all of her dirty clothes and towels. By now Katy had filled six large bags with trash and two with laundry. Then she dusted and polished, vacuumed, made her bed, and cleaned her bathroom until it sparkled. Finally, she dragged the trash bags out into the hall.

When she finished, she looked at the clock on her desk. It was almost noon. "I still have plenty of time to spend at Mrs. Piggle-Wiggle's house this afternoon working on the party decorations," Katy thought. "I can hardly wait to tell her the dream I had about my room last night. Mrs. Piggle-Wiggle loves to hear about all the kids' dreams and she really, really listens, too!"

Katy went to the top of the stairs and yelled down to her mother and father. "Mom, Dad, come see my room. No more messy stuffing and cramming, ever, ever again!"

SEVEN
The Never-Finish Cure

"**J**anie Beaumont, come back here this very minute! You are supposed to finish raking up these leaves," Mrs. Beaumont called.

But Janie didn't hear her mother. She was too busy yelling to her best friend, Christie Anne McClanahan, "Wait for me!" The rake lay forgotten in a lumpy pile of leaves as Janie leaped onto her bike and rode off down the street after Christie Anne.

About an hour later, the two girls, pink-cheeked and giggling, came bouncing into the kitchen, where Janie's mother had just taken a pan of muffins out of the oven.

"Oh goody, Mom," Janie said. "Can we have muffins and milk, please?"

It was difficult for Janie's mother to be stern with her daughter; she was always so sweet and enthusiastic.

"Oh, all right," said Mrs. Beaumont. "But you absolutely must finish raking up the leaves before dinnertime. You promised your father you would finish yesterday, you know."

"Sure, Mom. Hey, Christie Anne, you want to work on our bead rings?" asked Janie, reaching for a muffin. She took a big bite of muffin and ran for her box of beads. The girls sat at the kitchen table wolfing down snacks and stringing beads, chattering all the while.

Mrs. Beaumont went upstairs to make a phone call. She returned to the kitchen fifteen minutes later to find crumbs and beads scattered all over the table, and no girls in sight.

"Janie! Where did you go? Come back and clean up this mess."

But Janie and Christie Anne were nowhere to be seen. Mrs. Beaumont looked out the window, hoping to see Janie raking the yard, but the girls were not there either. Then she heard a shrill tooting noise coming from overhead. She tracked the sound to Janie's bedroom, where the girls were taking turns playing Janie's flute.

"Janie Beaumont," said her mother in exasperation, "you go right back downstairs and clean up your beads. And then you need to finish raking those leaves. I'm sorry, Christie Anne, but I think it's time for you to go home. Janie's got some work to do."

"Sorry, Mom," said Janie. "Bye, Christie Anne." She walked Christie Anne to the front door and then wandered into the kitchen, where she found half a muffin among the beads.

Absently nibbling it, Janie scooped up a handful of beads, fully intending to put them back in their storage box. But suddenly she spotted one of the rare sparkly teal beads that were her special favorites

It would be perfect for her new bead ring! Janie dropped the muffin and picked up the bead ring she'd begun earlier. She was hard at work on it when her mother came into the kitchen.

"Janie! I told you to clean up those beads! And you haven't finished the leaves yet. *And* you know you still have your book report to write. Mrs. McBride called me today to say this is the third time this month you have been late turning in your work. Now listen, darling, you've simply got to learn to finish things!"

"I'm sorry, Mom," said Janie remorsefully. "I guess I got distracted." She hurriedly scooped the rest of the beads (along with a good many muffin crumbs) into their box and ran upstairs to put the box away. She honestly meant to go back out and finish raking the leaves, as she had promised. But when she put the bead box on her desk, she saw the book that she was supposed to write her report on. She picked it up and flipped to a funny part she had especially liked. Before she knew it, she was deeply immersed in the book, which she had already read twice.

Suddenly a huge gust of wind blew a spattering of raindrops against the window. Janie jumped up from her bed and looked outside at the unraked leaves sailing through the air across the lawn and sidewalk.

"Oh well," she said. "I guess I'll finish raking tomorrow." But feeling a little nervous about what her mother would say, she decided to get going on her book report. She sat down at her desk and opened her drawer to get some paper. Her glance fell upon a bottle of her favorite glittery blue nail polish. She looked at her fingernails and forgot all about the book report.

She had just finished painting her left hand when the phone rang. It was Christie Anne, calling to talk about the costume party that the neighborhood children were throwing for Mrs. Piggle-Wiggle on her birthday. The girls were very excited about the party, and there were a great many important details to discuss. What kind of costumes would they wear? What kind of presents could they make for Mrs. Piggle-Wiggle? On and on the two girls giggled, planned, and gossiped until Janie heard her mother calling her to come down to dinner. Only then did Janie remember her still-unfinished book report.

She went into the kitchen, where her mother was making a salad and her father was opening the mail.

"Hi, Daddy," she said, somewhat sheepishly. "I'm sorry I didn't get those messy old leaves raked up before it began to rain."

Janie's father smiled at his little girl. "Well, your mother told me you were working on your book report, so I guess it's all right. How did it go? All finished?"

Janie gulped. "Well . . ."

"Janie," said her mother, eyeing her curiously, "why do you have nail polish on one hand and not the other?"

"Oh!" said Janie in surprise. "I guess I got distracted!"

Mr. and Mrs. Beaumont exchanged a glance.

"But you did finish the book report, didn't you?" Mrs. Beaumont asked.

"Well . . ." said Janie.

"I see," said her father. "All right, let's have dinner and then I strongly suggest you finish that report tonight—unless you'd like to be in the fourth grade until you're twelve," he added.

After dinner, Janie went dutifully up to her room. But when she picked up a pen to begin her book report, she noticed the unpolished nails on her right hand and decided to give them a quick coat first. Then she decided that she might as well paint her toes while she was at it. She sat on her bed to paint them, then once she was finished she realized she'd have to stay there until they were dry. Her pen and paper were out of reach, but she was just barely able to slide her bead box off the shelf.

"I'll just string a few beads while I'm waiting for the nail polish to dry," Janie thought.

She dug through the loose beads until she found the ring she had started earlier. Several of its beads had slipped off, because she had not tied off the string completely. Janie pawed through the box searching for the particular beads she wanted. She was so busy that she didn't hear her mother come into her room.

"That doesn't look like a book report to me," said Mrs. Beaumont. "I'm extremely disappointed in you, Janie. Now put those beads away this minute. It's way past your bedtime."

Janie looked up at her mother, stricken. "I'm sorry, Mom, honestly! I guess I just lost track of time. See, I was just going to——"

"Hush," interrupted her mother. "I'm tired of excuses. You'll have to get up early tomorrow and work on your book report before school."

Mrs. Beaumont kissed Janie good night and went downstairs, sighing heavily as she sank onto the couch beside her husband. Mr. Beaumont turned off the television and looked at her with one eyebrow raised.

"Don't tell me," he said. "She didn't finish?"

"I think she hardly even got started," moaned Mrs. Beaumont. "Oh, Hamilton, I don't know how to get Janie to finish *anything*! She is a very sweet and thoughtful girl, really very creative, but she just seems to drift from one project to the next, never finishing any of them."

"Have you talked to Christie Anne's mother?" asked Mr. Beaumont.

"Yes, and she says that Christie Anne is not

allowed to start a new project until she finishes the last one. But Janie always has so many projects under way, it could be years before she finishes them all!"

The next morning Janie's alarm went off very early. She got right up, intending to work on the long-neglected book report, but somewhere between her bed and her desk, she remembered Mrs. Piggle-Wiggle's party.

"Only four more days until the party!" she said. "I've got to get going on her present."

Janie loved to make things for people. She was especially excited about making a gift for Mrs. Piggle-Wiggle, because Mrs. Piggle-Wiggle was always so nice to her. She remembered how last summer she and some other children had wanted to play tug-of-war in Mrs. Piggle-Wiggle's yard. No one had a rope, so Mrs. Piggle-Wiggle had volunteered her red winter scarf. By the time Janie's team won the tug-of-war, pulling Blake Branson's team into the deep hole where the boys had been digging for Mr. Piggle-Wiggle's buried treasure, the poor red scarf had been stretched past all use. Now the cold weather was coming, thought Janie, and Mrs. Piggle-Wiggle had no scarf.

"That's what I'll do, I'll knit her one."

She took the knitting basket out of her closet and cleared her desk to make room for it. Then she began to sort through the yarn, picking out colors. When her mother called her to breakfast, she jumped. Time had slipped away so quickly! Janie hurried into her clothes and made her bed. She raced downstairs to the kitchen, thinking of nothing but Mrs. Piggle-Wiggle's scarf.

"Good morning," greeted her father. "How's that book report coming along?"

Janie gasped. "Oh! I was just about to start when I remembered that I need a gift for Mrs. Piggle-Wiggle's party this weekend, and—"

"There will be no party for you, young lady," said Mr. Beaumont sternly, "unless you finish that book report."

"And rake the leaves," added Mrs. Beaumont.

"Okay," said Janie in a pitiful little voice. She looked so miserable that Mrs. Beaumont softened a bit. After Janie had left for school, her mother sat musing about her sweet-natured daughter. Surely it wasn't Janie's fault, she thought, that she was so easily distracted. But really, that book report was almost a week overdue by now!

Just then the phone rang. It was the Beaumonts' next-door neighbor, Phyllis Philpot. Mrs. Beaumont had barely gotten out a hello when Phyllis started talking.

"Mary Louise, I hate to bother you but Sinclair and I are very concerned about the leaves that have begun to blow into our yard. As you know, Carrie and Larry have mold allergies, and . . ."

"Yes, I know all about the twins' allergies," said Mrs. Beaumont hastily. "Janie will finish raking the leaves this afternoon."

"Oh, good, because otherwise I'm afraid I'm going to have to start putting masks on the twins before they go outside, and really that would be awful, because their skin is so very sensitive, you know . . ."

"Yes, yes, awful," murmured Mrs. Beaumont, getting off the phone as fast as she could. But the problem of Janie's distractibility worried her more than ever. It was bad enough to think that Janie might have to miss Mrs. Piggle-Wiggle's birthday party, but now she had to put up with Phyllis Philpot's complaining, too!

Thinking of Mrs. Piggle-Wiggle gave Mrs. Beaumont an idea. She dialed Mrs. Piggle-Wiggle's number and explained the whole situation.

"I'm certainly glad you called, Mrs. Beaumont," said Mrs. Piggle-Wiggle. "I would hate for Janie to miss my birthday just as much as you would. I'm counting on her to help with the decorations— she has such a creative touch, you know. Let's see, I think this calls for a dose of accomplishment powder."

"Accomplishment powder?" echoed Mrs. Beaumont.

"Yes, indeed. All you do is sprinkle a little on Janie's hands and feet after she goes to sleep tonight. Shall I send it over? Wag can deliver it."

"Oh, yes, please! Thank you so much, Mrs. Piggle-Wiggle."

By the time Janie came home from school that day, Wag had dropped off the accomplishment powder and Mrs. Beaumont had tucked it away in the medicine cabinet. Mrs. Beaumont waited anxiously for her daughter's bedtime to arrive. She had to remind Janie at least half a dozen times to finish raking the leaves; Janie kept starting the task with a good will, but after a few minutes her attention wandered. At one point Mrs. Beaumont caught her with the rake in one hand and a book in the other, trying to read and gather leaves at the same time, and accomplishing very little of either. Mrs. Beaumont shook her head in exasperation, but she said nothing.

She also said nothing when Janie got busy knitting instead of working on her book report, nor when Janie drifted away from the knitting—leaving a tangle of rainbow-colored yarn on her desk— to pull out half the contents of her mother's craft closet in search of the materials she needed to make her costume for Mrs. Piggle-Wiggle's party.

Mr. Beaumont looked as if *he* could say plenty when he came home and found the leaves still strewn all over the yard, but Mrs. Beaumont shushed him and told him in a whisper all about the accomplishment powder.

"Better make it a double dose," muttered Mr. Beaumont, eyeing the trail of Janie's unfinished projects.

That evening, when Mrs. Beaumont was sure Janie was fast asleep, she tiptoed to her bedside and carefully sprinkled the powder on Janie's hands and feet. It was almost invisible, just a faint dusty glimmering in the dim hall light.

The next morning Janie got up and began to make her bed, just like always. Then she caught sight of her knitting on the desk, and the heap of yarn. She thought of how happy Mrs. Piggle-Wiggle would be with her rainbow scarf, and she felt a rush of enthusiasm to work on the scarf right away. She turned toward the desk but found, much to her surprise, that her feet would not move away from the bed and her hands would not let go of the bedsheet. She shook her arms, trying to open her hands, but they clutched the sheet tightly and would not let go.

"Mom!" she yelled in alarm. Her mother came running.

"What is it?"

"I can't stop making my bed!" Janie wailed.

Mrs. Beaumont laughed. "Good for you," she said, heading on down the hall.

"Wait, Mom, you don't understand—" called Janie, while her hands, seeming to work all on their own, as if they were not parts of her body, pulled the sheet to the head of the bed and smoothed it down. They went on pulling and patting and smoothing until the comforter was properly spread and the pillow fluffed. Only then was Janie able to move away from the bed. She sank down in her desk chair in relief to write her book report.

There was still time before breakfast to work on the scarf, she decided. She made a move to shove her half-finished book report out of the way so that she could work on Mrs. Piggle-Wiggle's scarf, but to her great consternation, she found that she could not let go of the paper.

"Not again!" she wailed.

After several attempts to drop the paper, shake it loose, and even hurl it across the room, all to no avail, Janie sighed and decided she might as well write her book report and get it over with. She reached for a pen. This time her hands obeyed instantly. Shrugging, Janie began to write. Once she started, she found that she could not stop. She wrote and wrote, and before she knew it, the report was finished. Only then would her busy hand release the pen.

"Well, that's done, at least," she said, but now her mother was calling her down to breakfast, and there was no time to work on the scarf. She scrambled into her clothes and brushed her hair. Her hands cooperated beautifully, except when she tried to put the brush down halfway through.

It was like that all day long. Janie found herself unable to fiddle with her bracelet during math class, or to write a note to Christie Anne during science. At lunchtime, she even had to finish her sandwich before her hands would let her pick up a cookie.

At recess, all the kids were talking about Mrs. Piggle-Wiggle's party. Janie couldn't wait to get home and work on her costume—not to mention Mrs. Piggle-Wiggle's scarf. That afternoon, she ran home as fast as she could. She kicked her way through the leaves that covered her lawn. But when she tried to run up the porch steps, she discovered that her feet would not budge from the walkway and her hands were reaching for the rake, which she had left lying in the grass the day before.

It was Mrs. Beaumont's turn to be surprised when she glanced out the window, wondering why Janie hadn't come home from school yet, and saw her daughter industriously raking the last of the leaves into a huge pile in the side yard. With a final flourish of the rake, Janie turned and ran toward the kitchen door, red-cheeked and breathless.

"Look, Mom! I finished the leaves! Now I just need to bag them before they blow away."

"Don't you want to come in for a snack first?" asked her bewildered mother.

"No, I'll just finish this job first, okay?"

When Janie finished bagging the leaves, her hands wouldn't let go of the leaf bag until she tied the bag shut. She was going to leave the rake leaning against the fence, but her hands wouldn't let go of the handle until she hung the rake up in the garage where it belonged.

"All finished, Mom," Janie announced proudly as

she ran into the kitchen. "I need to take my snack up to my room because I've got a lot of stuff to finish before the party tomorrow."

Janie's mother gave her a big hug. "Your father will be very happy when he sees what a beautiful job you did raking up all the leaves."

Janie hurried up the stairs two at a time, and when she went into her room she started toward the phone by her bed to call Christie Anne, but her feet marched her past the bed and she sat down at her desk instead. She tried to reach for the bead box but her hands fastened on a twist of rainbow yarn and then on her knitting needles. When the phone by Janie's bed rang, she tried to stand up but she was stuck to the chair. She couldn't let go of the yarn, but she found that she didn't even mind, because she could hardly wait to finish the scarf for Mrs. Piggle-Wiggle. And once she began to knit, Janie was so excited to watch it grow ever longer that she didn't even try to start anything else until the scarf was finished.

Once she tied off the last bit of rainbow-colored fringe, Janie realized that she had plenty of time before dinner to work on her costume, too.

Janie began putting her dancing princess costume together. Her mother had saved Janie's ballerina skirt from the spring dance recital, and as Janie rummaged through the pile of things she had found in her mother's craft closet, she said to herself, "The hem of the skirt could use a few sparkly beads." When she reached for the bead box, she saw the unfinished beaded ring. She thought about picking up the ring, but she decided to finish her costume first. Janie carefully glued two rows of sparkly beads on the hem of the ballerina skirt. Then, with no trouble, she finished not only the bead ring, but a matching bracelet and necklace as well.

Looking at the finished jewelry, Janie realized that it would match her dancing princess costume perfectly. She decided to try everything on to see how it looked.

"Wow, this is beautiful!" Janie said proudly. She pirouetted in front of the mirror, admiring all she had accomplished. "Now I'm finished, and I'm all ready for Mrs. Piggle-Wiggle's birthday party!"

EIGHT

Mrs. Piggle-Wiggle's Birthday Party

It was Wag who heard the children first. He jumped up from his resting spot in the warm sunshine streaming through the bedroom window and began barking excitedly, wagging his tail back and forth.

"Yes, Wag, I hear them too." Mrs. Piggle-Wiggle smiled. She hurried downstairs and opened the front door wide.

"What a lovely day this promises to be!" she exclaimed as she stood in the sunlight watching all of her young friends scamper toward her upside-down house.

Up the street, skipping, waving, laughing, and calling to each other, came the children. Some were on roller skates, some on bicycles, some on skateboards and scooters. And all were carrying bags of brightly colored decorations. A few children even pulled along wagons full of colorfully wrapped packages.

The first ones up the front steps were Janie Beaumont and Christie Anne McClanahan, smiling and out of breath from their skate.

"Happy Birthday, Mrs. Piggle-Wiggle!" they shouted in unison. "What a wonderful day you've picked to celebrate your birthday! It's a good thing we baked so many cakes and cupcakes yesterday! It looks like *everyone* is coming to your birthday party!"

Blake Branson put his bags of decorations on the porch steps and hung his costume on the porch railing, saying proudly, "Mom and Dad and a bunch of the other parents are sending you a surprise today 'cause it's your birthday."

"Shhhh, silly! You'll spoil it!" the girls said.

Mrs. Piggle-Wiggle just smiled and gave Blake a big hug. "That's so sweet of them, dear! Now, children, let's get busy. You girls can help me in the house with the food. Boys, I found some sawhorses and planks in the basement that will make the perfect party tables and benches."

Patsy Waters and Betsy Applebee, who had just skipped into the front hall, said in unison, "Don't you dare! No work for you today, Mrs. Piggle-Wiggle. We'll take care of everything. Now you just sit and relax." Betsy pulled out a chair.

Soon everyone was busy. Blake helped Ricky and Woody Timbers drag the sawhorses and planks up from the basement and made a long table with benches under the apple tree.

"Whoa, Blake," said Woody. "For a minute I thought you were going to let the cat out of the bag and tell Mrs. Piggle-Wiggle what her surprise is."

Will Pemberton dragged Mrs. Piggle-Wiggle's rocking chair off the front porch and put it at the head of the table. Sharon Rogers and Marilyn Matson decorated the chairs with balloons and streamers.

"We had better fill in a few of those holes we dug

yesterday when we were looking for treasure, or one of the clumsy old girls will fall in," said Timmy O'Connor with a smirk on his face.

"That's not very nice, Timmy. Mrs. Piggle-Wiggle wouldn't want you to say such mean things," said Blake as he picked up a shovel and began to fill in a particularly deep hole by the apple tree.

"That's right!" said Marilyn. "Besides, you're probably just worried that we girls will find your old treasure before you do!"

"Hey, down below," yelled Sean Hanover from up in the top of the tree. "Quit blabbing and blow up some more balloons!"

"Yeah!" shouted George O'Connor, who was just a branch below Sean. "Stop all that chin music. We need a ton more balloons up here and lots more streamers to tie 'em up."

"What's chin music, George?" asked Hubert Prentiss as he hoisted himself onto the next branch over.

"That's what my dad says to my mom when she talks on the phone too long," George replied.

There were at least six boys in the apple tree, and

at its base were eight red-faced balloon blowers with yards of colored streamers draped over their shoulders. Matt and Kevin McGregor were winding the bright paper ribbons around the trunk and tying balloons to the lower branches. Matt made sure Mrs. Piggle-Wiggle wasn't in earshot, then, just to be safe, he shielded his mouth with one hand and loudly whispered to Kevin and the balloon blowers, "My big brother, Richard, told me that everything is all set for the big S-U-R-P-R-I-S-E!"

In the kitchen, Mrs. Piggle-Wiggle smiled and hummed along to the music of tapping hammers and popping staplers as every picket of the fence surrounding her yard was decorated. Streamers, banners, and balloons were soon merrily flying from every surface that could be hammered, tied, stapled, or draped. Clusters of balloons and streamers danced in the breeze as it blew softly through the branches of the apple tree.

The party table and benches were draped in a lumpy excess of colored paper stapled heavily in place. The girls had decorated Mrs. Piggle-Wiggle's rocking chair with so many balloons that one leg hovered inches above the ground, threatening to fly away. And on the front porch, Penelope's cage was covered with flowers and streamers, and Penelope herself squawked "Happy Birthday! Happy Birthday!" whenever any of the children walked past.

The whole house teemed with busy decorators endlessly whispering about a birthday surprise. The children exchanged smug smiles whenever they passed each other, proud that Mrs. Piggle-Wiggle did not have the foggiest idea what on earth the surprise could be. The kitchen was filled with choruses of "oopsies" and lots of laughter as the girls spread frosting and sprinkled candy on the enormous eight-layer birthday cake. Finally, the cake was assembled and decorated. The happy bakers anchored the layers with long wooden skewers to keep the huge cake from toppling over under the weight of the swirls and blobs of rainbow-colored frosting that had been lavishly applied, and the cake now sat regally, covered in shiny red foil, on Mrs. Piggle-Wiggle's breadboard.

Mrs. Piggle-Wiggle's largest soup pots acted as punchbowls, filled to the brim with pink lemonade. Every bowl and basket in her kitchen held popcorn, potato chips, and candy, and two whole dishpans were filled with fruit salad. Paper plates, napkins, and cups, and plastic forks and spoons, were already set out on the long picnic table.

"Let's carry the dining room table outside and use it to put all this lovely food on," Mrs. Piggle-Wiggle suggested, smiling at her eager helpers. And of course she didn't say a word as she crunched her way across the sticky, gooey, kitchen floor.

"I think we're ready to eat. What do you think, Lester?" she asked.

Lester the pig, who had been doing his best to wipe up the dripping frosting and push the spilled decorations into neat piles, nodded eagerly.

"Mrs. Piggle-Wiggle," Betsy Applebee said, "how many candles shall we put on your cake?"

Now as you might remember, no one really knew how old Mrs. Piggle-Wiggle was nor how old she would be if today really *were* her birthday.

"The more the merrier, Betsy dear, but I think twenty seems like a nice round number to me. What do you girls think?"

The girls all agreed happily that twenty was an excellent number.

"Now, Lester dear, please help me slide the birthday cake onto the tea wagon and I'll let you put the candles on for me." Lester carefully placed twenty-two candles neatly on the huge cake. "Oh, Lester, thank you, how clever of you. Twenty candles and two extra. One candle to make a wish on and one to grow!" Mrs. Piggle-Wiggle laughed as she said, "Of course, I will never grow any bigger."

Just then, Blake Branson and Will Pemberton came racing into the kitchen, skidding to a stop just before hitting the towering birthday cake. "There's a pizza truck and an ice cream truck outside. They say that they have a present for you!" Everyone ran outside to the front yard to see.

"Hello, gentlemen," Mrs. Piggle-Wiggle said with a smile. "What can I do for you?"

The pizza man spoke first. "Well, ma'am, we heard that you were having a birthday party today, and we've brought pizza and ice cream for everyone!"

With that, the children let up a cheer.

"Compliments of all of the parents in the neighborhood, with their thanks," the ice cream man added with a wink.

"Why, what a wonderful surprise!" Mrs. Piggle-Wiggle clapped her hands together in delight. Everyone filled their plates with all the pizza and ice cream they could eat, and headed to the picnic tables to fill their tummies as well.

The children had piled their presents for Mrs. Piggle-Wiggle in the shiny new red wheelbarrow they had bought with their saved allowances, and had hidden the wheelbarrow under a tarp in the backyard. Now it sat gleaming proudly by Mrs. Piggle-Wiggle's rocking chair, full of gaily wrapped packages.

Kitten Hanover led Mrs. Piggle-Wiggle to her rocking chair. "Keep your eyes closed and don't open them until we tell you to," she warned. After Mrs. Piggle-Wiggle was seated, the children all said in unison, "NOW, open your eyes!" and launched into a spirited rendition of "Happy Birthday," with Fetlock Harroway singing so enthusiastically that he kept going for a few lines even after everyone else had finished.

Mrs. Piggle-Wiggle clapped her hands and beamed. "That was lovely, children! Thank you!"

The boys sat on one side of the long table and the girls on the other, with Mrs. Piggle-Wiggle at the head of the table and Lester at the other end. Penelope was uncovered and happily eating fruit salad, occasionally squawking, "Happy birthday! Awk! Happy birthday!" Wag sat under the table hoping for scraps to fall, while Lightfoot slept on her pillow on the porch. Jonathan Campbell had tied Spotty the pony under the apple tree, where he could watch the party and of course enjoy the carrots Jonathan had thoughtfully brought for him.

Soon all the food was eaten and Jonathan announced proudly, "Time to open your presents, Mrs. Piggle-Wiggle."

"More presents? Why children, you shouldn't have! Oh my, what a grand party we're having, but I think we should get into our costumes before I open these lovely packages. Let's wheel everything in and put it next to the chandelier and the birthday cake."

Everyone helped clear the table. The wheelbar-row was put next to the chandelier, which was already lit up in order to show off more decorations. One of the dining room chairs had been decorated to resemble a throne for Mrs. Piggle-Wiggle.

"Fit for a queen," Christy Anne said proudly as she draped the chair with a white fake fur blanket that she had brought from home.

"Please, please, Mrs. Piggle-Wiggle, open your presents now! We're too excited to wait till costume time," said Molly O'Toole, hopping up and down with excitement.

"Yes, please open them!" said the children as they gathered around Mrs. Piggle-Wiggle's chair.

"Read the card tied to the wheelbarrow first," Sean said. Mrs. Piggle-Wiggle carefully opened the card and read aloud.

"From all of us. Happy Birthday!"

Each child had signed his or her name below.

"Thank you, children!" Mrs. Piggle-Wiggle said. "What a wonderful surprise, a beautiful new wheel-barrow! I'll bet you boys have tried to repair that old worn-out, leaky tire on my old one a million times. This is the perfect gift!"

Then Mrs. Piggle-Wiggle opened each present and read each card. Soon there was a huge pile of wrapping paper in the wheelbarrow, and a pile of opened presents next to it—new garden tools from Kitty Wheeling, a handmade pot holder from Pergola Wingsproggle, dish towels from Molly O'Toole, garden gloves, a new gardening hat, a rainbow-colored scarf, an apron, and, finally, a scrapbook filled with pictures of all the children.

Mrs. Piggle-Wiggle had tears in her eyes and a smile on her lips as she thanked each child. "Thank you, boys and girls. You are my dearest and best friends, and you have given me so much happiness today. Now it's time for costumes and the birthday cake. Boys, take your costumes upstairs into the spare room. Girls, you can change in my room and then you can help me decide what to wear."

Everyone raced up the stairs. There was a lot of good-natured bumping and shoving, but Mrs. Piggle-Wiggle didn't hear a single cross word as she followed the jostling children, Wag at her heels.

Soon all the girls had on their costumes. They could hear the boys clattering and banging as they raced back downstairs. "Hurry, Mrs. Piggle-Wiggle. What are you going to wear? The boys are all dressed," they pleaded.

"Yes, I can hear them. Close your eyes and count to twenty slowly." Mrs. Piggle-Wiggle chuckled to herself as she went into her closet. "I know what I'll wear now—my queen outfit! That will be just perfect for today, for you have all made me feel just like a queen."

When the girls had slowly counted to twenty, they opened their eyes. There stood Mrs. Piggle-Wiggle, resplendently dressed. She had on a lavender satin dress and around her shoulders she had draped a purple fur-trimmed robe. Atop her head glittered a jeweled crown. She wore gold slippers with jeweled buckles on her feet and rings on every finger. As a final touch, she carried a gold scepter.

"Oh, Mrs. Piggle-Wiggle, you look beautiful!" the girls exclaimed as they gathered around her.

"Come, my loyal subjects, down to the throne room to join the others," Mrs. Piggle-Wiggle said in her most queenly voice. "Follow me."

Two ballerinas held Mrs. Piggle-Wiggle's train as the rest of the costumed little girls followed them down the stairs.

No one said a word until Mrs. Piggle-Wiggle was seated. Holding the golden scepter high, she said, "Now, let me have a look at my loyal subjects' costumes."

There were many sparkly ballerinas and princesses, five gypsies, two mermaids, and one cowgirl. The boys had mostly dressed as pirates and cowboys. There were two clowns, an astronaut, and a deep-sea diver. At the back of the crowd of children hid three boys who clearly did not want to be seen.

"Step forward, my three loyal subjects. Be not afraid," Mrs. Piggle-Wiggle said in her most queenly voice.

Jonathan Campbell and the two little McGregor twins, Kevin and Matt, walked slowly forward. None of them were wearing costumes.

"Why, what is the problem, my subjects? Why do you look so sad?" Mrs. Piggle-Wiggle asked.

"We forgot our costumes," little Kevin McGregor said sadly, looking down at the floor.

"Why, that is no problem at all!" said Mrs. Piggle-Wiggle, walking over to a large, intricately carved Chinese chest under the living room window. "This is a perfect time to open the magic chest.

"Now," she said majestically as she swirled aside the Spanish shawl that covered the chest, "I think my three loyal subjects will find what they need in here. Come, Jonathan, and bring Matt and Kevin with you."

Mrs. Piggle-Wiggle pointed at the brass lock with her scepter as she handed Jonathan the large gold key on a heavy gold chain that she wore looped over the gold belt around her waist. Jonathan proudly took the key and knelt down in front of the chest.

"Wow, this is way cool!" Jonathan said, his eyes wide as saucers. "There are so many costumes in here. Look, Matt and Kevin!"

The three boys each found just what they wanted to wear and hurried upstairs to put on their costumes. While they were waiting for them, the other children took turns looking in the huge magic costume chest. Soon everyone had found at least two or three things to add to their costumes. Sparkly wands, gold-painted wooden swords, assorted jewelry and tiaras, feather boas, silver and gold slippers, boots and capes, flower-covered hats, fringed leather vests, complete ballerina costumes, pirate costumes, cowboy hats, and even a dragon and a gorilla suit.

Once they had finished outfitting themselves, the children turned to Mrs. Piggle-Wiggle's pets. Before long, Wag was wearing a red silk scarf and Lightfoot a pale blue one. Lester looked dashing, if a bit uncomfortable, in a purple velvet vest and a white sequined bow tie.

The children were still looking through the costumes scattered around the chest when Jonathan, Matt, and Kevin came back downstairs dressed as swashbuckling pirates.

"Now, my loyal subjects, are you all ready to eat cake?" Mrs. Piggle-Wiggle said.

"Yes!"

"You bet!"

"Let's dig in!"

"Then let us close the magic chest and retire to the feast," Mrs. Piggle-Wiggle intoned regally.

The children began picking up the costumes

from the floor and handing them to Jonathan, who placed them carefully into the chest. Suddenly he stopped, a startled look on his face, and began rummaging in the bottom of the trunk. "Hey, Mrs. Piggle-Wiggle, I think I found something!" Jonathan said. "There's a funny lump in the bottom." He rummaged a bit more. "Here it is!" he exclaimed. "It's some sort of knob."

Jonathan pulled on the knob, but nothing happened. He began emptying the costumes once again, diving further and further into the deep chest. "I'd better take the rest of these out, Mrs. Piggle-Wiggle," Jonathan said in a muffled voice. He was now hanging upside down over the side of the chest, handing the remaining costumes to Matt and Kevin, who were piling them on the floor. When the chest was empty, Matt and Kevin grabbed Jonathan's feet, and he put both hands on the knob and gave a hard yank.

All of a sudden the children heard a muffled "Whoa!" from the bottom of the chest. They ran and peered over the sides just in time to see the floor of the chest slowly slide to one side, revealing a hidden compartment. "Mrs. Piggle-Wiggle, look!" Jonathan said proudly, staring into the dark recesses of the newly unveiled secret compartment.

"Why, Jonathan, I never knew there was a hidden false bottom in this chest," Mrs. Piggle-Wiggle said. Jonathan raised his head from the chest and stepped out of the way to allow Mrs. Piggle-Wiggle a closer look. She reached in and took out a large package wrapped in red satin, tied with a gold ribbon. There was a small white card attached, which she read aloud:

Dear Wife,

Happy Birthday, finally, my love. I knew that you would choose to celebrate your birthday someday, and knowing how much you and your young friends love to play dress-up, I thought it would be fun to hide this grand present for you in your costume trunk. Much Joy!

Your loving husband,
Captain Piggle-Wiggle

Mrs. Piggle-Wiggle opened the package. There were stacks and stacks of seed packets—seeds for every kind of flower and herb and vegetable that the children had ever heard of—and some that they hadn't. There was a gold envelope nestled among the treasure. She opened it and out fell another note, as well as a large, folded blue paper. Mrs. Piggle-Wiggle read the note aloud:

Dear Wife,

Now you can have the vegetable garden that we always talked about. As you can see, there are seeds enough for you to plant the biggest, best garden ever. I am also giving you the set of blueprints for that treehouse that you always wanted to build in the apple tree. Before my last journey, I left instructions at the hardware store, so they will have everything you need. Enjoy the garden and treehouse, and think of me.

Happy Birthday once again,
Your loving husband

"Oh, children, isn't this a lovely birthday surprise!" Mrs. Piggle-Wiggle said, tears of joy streaming down her face. "Now we must really celebrate and light the birthday candles."

Mrs. Piggle-Wiggle waved the gold scepter over the cake and each candle magically burst to life. "Now," Mrs. Piggle-Wiggle said in her queenly voice, "blow out the candles for me, loyal subjects, and make a wish for yourselves, as all of *my* birthday wishes have come true."

Once the candles were blown out, Janie Beaumont and Christie Anne McClanahan began cutting the cake and handing out slices. The festive group fell silent for a few moments, as they happily devoured their treats. Mrs. Piggle-Wiggle and the children had just about finished when Matt nudged Kevin and whispered, "I think I hear them coming up the street."

"Who?" Kevin asked. Matt nudged him.

"Ohhhh." Kevin nodded in understanding. "Yahoo!" he shouted as he ran and opened the front door. "Come on outside, Mrs. Piggle-Wiggle, your surprise is here!"

"Another surprise!" Mrs. Piggle-Wiggle exclaimed.

"But you've already given me the loveliest birthday anyone has ever had. What else could there possibly be?"

Mrs. Piggle-Wiggle followed Matt to the door with all the other children jostling, jumping up and down, and joyously shouting behind them. As Mrs. Piggle-Wiggle stepped out onto the front porch, she gasped, for waiting in the street outside her house was an entire marching band. And when they saw her, they immediately struck up "For She's a Jolly Good Fellow!"

"Surprise, surprise, Mrs. Piggle-Wiggle! Happy surprise birthday parade!" the children shouted above the music.

Mrs. Piggle-Wiggle could not believe her eyes and ears. "Oh my goodness, how splendid! Thank you, thank you. Why, this is the grandest and most wonderful surprise of all. I do love a parade!"

"Come on, Mrs. Piggle-Wiggle! They're waiting for us!" Matt said, grabbing her hand and dragging her to the street.

When they reached the end of the walk, the

band leader strode over to them. He bowed to Mrs. Piggle-Wiggle and held out his hand with a grin. With a bewildered look, Mrs. Piggle-Wiggle placed her hand in his and followed him. He brought her to the rear of the band, where Spotty the pony waited, wearing a festive, flower-bedecked saddle. The band leader escorted Mrs. Piggle-Wiggle to Spotty, helped her into the saddle, and then resumed his place at the front of the band. At his signal, and still playing merrily, the band began to march down the street. As the band moved forward, the children formed two lines on either side of Spotty and marched along, raising their knees high with every step.

And with that, the entire parade marched proudly down the streets of town. Parents and well-wishers lined the streets, some holding banners saying "We love you, Mrs. Piggle-Wiggle!" and others waving flags. Everyone was whistling and clapping along to the music, and shouts of "Happy Birthday, Mrs. Piggle-Wiggle!" followed the happy costumed marchers all the way through town.

By the time the parade arrived at the town square

the whole town was there. The mayor himself escorted Mrs. Piggle-Wiggle from her perch atop Spotty to a throne in the large gazebo in the square. And when the band began playing "Happy Birthday," an enormous circle formed around Mrs. Piggle-Wiggle as the town joined in joyful voice to serenade her.

THE END

Betty MacDonald (1908–1958) was the author of the beloved books about Mrs. Piggle-Wiggle: MRS. PIGGLE-WIGGLE; HELLO, MRS. PIGGLE-WIGGLE; MRS. PIGGLE-WIGGLE'S MAGIC; and MRS. PIGGLE-WIGGLE'S FARM. The Mrs. Piggle-Wiggle stories were first told to her two daughters.

After Betty MacDonald's death, her daughter **Anne MacDonald Canham** found a never-before-published Mrs. Piggle-Wiggle story along with notes for other stories among her mother's possessions. This was the beginning of HAPPY BIRTHDAY, MRS. PIGGLE-WIGGLE, the first new Mrs. Piggle-Wiggle book in fifty years.

Alexandra Boiger is the illustrator of WHILE MAMA HAD A QUICK LITTLE CHAT and ROXIE AND THE HOOLIGANS. She lives in San Anselmo, California. You can visit her online at www.alexandraboiger.com.